SILVER DREAM RACER

John Lydecker

Silver Dream Racer

A novelization based upon
a screenplay by David Wickes

Futura Publications Limited

A Futura Book

First published in Great Britain by
Futura Publications Limited in 1980

ISBN 0 7088 1762 9

Filmset, printed and bound in Great Britain
by Hazell Watson & Viney Ltd
Aylesbury, Bucks

Futura Publications Limited
110 Warner Road
Camberwell, London SE5

PROLOGUE

The Range Rover sat alone in the deserted quarry, a low trailer empty and waiting behind it. Both of the car's doors were open to let the warm June air blow through, carrying with it the stale grey dust of the chalk bits. But it was bearable; better than the stuffy heat of closed windows. There was a girl in the car – well, she thought as she knocked the rearview mirror around, maybe not so much a girl any more. Those laugh lines were beginning to get a little etched, but what the hell, she'd rather have a couple of lines at thirty than a smooth skin and a sour nature.

She was listening to the radio, but outside, the air was filled with the hornet's drone of two trail bikes as they circled and sported beyond the lip of the quarry. Her name was Tina; Christina her mother had called her because it sounded regal, Chrissie they'd called her at school because it somehow suited the hockey team captain, and Tina as Greg called her because it was short, affectionate and easy to live with.

Greg and Terry were out there now, rough biking – nothing competitive, just a scramble around the pits and the scrub-covered piles of waste for the sheer joy of riding. Tina had begged off from the actual scrambling. She didn't ride, and a pillion passenger under such conditions could be disastrous. They'd started with a fast turn along the old road, racing up to where the empty shells of the old quarry buildings stood, then making a fast turn which sent dust and stones flying in a high arc, to come spattering down as a dry rain. Terry led as they made for the basin, Greg followed and hung back to avoid the blinding storm of grit

5

that was at its worst where the chalk was powdery and soft.

The two bikes had disappeared from Tina's view, only the high wail of their engines giving any indication of where they were. She tried to follow by sound alone, but the sun was in her eyes and the echoes were deceptive; now and again she could see them as they crested one hummock or another, wrenching the handlebars to get some grip on the sparse vegetation that held the slag together.

Tina fished her trainers from under the seat and pulled them on, then she began the short climb to the edge of the quarry.

When she looked down into the basin with its terraced cliffs, she got the impression that a medium-size mountain had been scooped out of the land, leaving an open scar that showed only the merest traces of beginning to heal, as coarse grass got a hold on the loose material at its foot. The mound had slumped and eroded into a series of dunes, and it was here that Greg and Terry were riding.

There was a ridge of soft limestone that had grown too big to hold together; its inward-side breaking into a clifflike slope, overhung with matted roots of tenacious scrub on its crest. There was another cliff facing it, a little lower, and angled towards it like a ramp. They formed a miniature canyon between them, quite spectacular in its way. Terry was storming along the lower of the two rises, coming dangerously close to the edge; his slewing stop would have to be spectacular to prevent himself from going over the edge. Greg was wisely hanging back, staying well clear of the upflung dustcloud that Terry was trailing.

He was leaving it too late to stop, getting too close to the crumbling lip of the cliff, even accelerating as he came nearer; then he was over the side, descending the steep wall of the canyon in a controlled scramble, and Greg was coming in to follow.

Terry crossed the canyon at a diagonal and gunned his machine at the opposite wall. It was thirty, perhaps even forty feet high, and so steep that it couldn't be far from the vertical. Greg was hammering down the ridges dug by Terry's wheels, as Terry used the raw power of his machine to drag him up the impossible incline, helping with his feet whenever the grip of the tyres didn't seem to be enough. For a moment, as he neared the crest, it seemed that the bike was clinging like a fly with some mysterious adhesion that prevented it from falling backwards; and then, with a twist of the throttle and a roar from the engine, Terry was over the lip and speeding away, both wheels clear of the edge and biting on safe ground as the bike gunned forward.

Greg was trying to follow, already halfway up but having difficulty with the sheer wall. He gave a burst of throttle and the bike leaped forward, but for the few feet that he gained he began to lose his front wheel as it came away from the face and started to arc back. The wheel continued to lift as he fought to push it down, but he had no leverage. Suddenly the whole bike tipped backwards and started to drop.

The crest was still several feet above but the machine turned almost completely over. Greg was starting to fall away from the saddle, unable to retain a grip on the bucking machine.

Greg hit the chalk first; then the bike crashed on top of him, its wheels still spinning. Tina was already running, forgetful of her own safety, and Terry, no longer able to hear his friend's machine, was turning and making his way around the broken heap. Tina was the first to arrive with Terry close behind. He flung his own bike aside and jumped in to wrench the heavy frame from the fallen rider.

The grey chalk was soaking up the blood as fast as Greg's twisted body could pump it out. But after a few minutes there was nothing left to absorb except for Tina's cascading tears.

ONE

It's a deathwish; at least, that's what it's been called. Anybody who dedicates his life to the angry and powerful machines that are racing motorcycles must be motivated by something other than the wish for money and fame. Tough as he may be, the metal is always tougher, and has no fear. Hesitation and miscalculation at speeds nearing two hundred miles per hour, lead within seconds to severe or permanent injury. Sometimes you win and sometimes you lose, but if you lose it's because you didn't measure up, and if you don't measure up – what's the point in being alive?

Say it to a rider and he'll probably shrug, maybe even agree with you. For him it's no great discovery, no new insight, simply a restatement of the hard and uncompromising principles by which he lives and which only another rider, one of the brotherhood of danger, can ever fully understand. They know what it is to run near the edge, to feel the elation of fear and live with the nearness of death. For some people it's a special kind of madness but for the riders it's the only kind of life they want.

Spills, they are euphemistically termed; those tearing, frightening slides of body and machine at high speeds which can follow error, collision or seizure. Donington Park had seen its share of broken collarbones, ribs and fingers, compressed vertebrae and concussions, snapped limbs, strained muscles and hemorrhages. None of these would discourage a rider for long – within weeks he'd be back, strapped, bandaged and dosed with painkillers, ready to compete again.

There wasn't much of a crowd that day, well short of the fifty thousand or more that could be attracted to a major competition. This was small-league stuff, mainly under-financed privateers and garage-sponsored outfits, and it was difficult to see why the huge Trans-World operation troubled to turn up at all; the prize money would barely cover their expenses in bringing up the fleet of backup vehicles and the small army of mechanics, press agents, photographers and management staff. But nobody was going to turn them away, not when they fielded a team which was headed by Bruce McBride, the golden boy and self-proclaimed ass-hole of world-class racing.

McBride was over from the USA for the European track season, grabbing the headlines not only with his wins – which were frequent and spectacular – but also with his arrogant self-assurance, a grandstanding showmanship that couldn't antagonize, because it was so open and exuberant. The two backup riders on the team, Nichols and Mendoza, supported the image with a line in irreverent crosstalk and appalling vaudeville jokes, that guaranteed them the centre-stage at any gathering.

McBride had got a bad start and was lying second to Nick Freeman, as the fast-moving pack began to spread out in the third lap. Freeman's yellow Yamaha had been described by one perceptive critic as a lawnmower: a collection of cannibalized spares held together more by strong will than engineering, and certainly no match for McBride's finely-tuned and first-class Suzuki; but Freeman had the lead and he was holding it, hugging the inside line on Donington's sweeping bends and leaving McBride no gap to storm through.

Freeman pressed close to his machine, as the leading group emerged from the bend and into the long straight with hardly any space between them. He didn't need to look back to know that McBride was there, close behind, poised for any opportunity as they righted themselves rapidly after leaning into the curve and accelerated to take the greatest advantage of this open stretch. McBride could beat him for speed, but he would have to take the risk of leaving himself out of line for the next curve so that he would be forced to fall back or spin off; Freeman held his position and willed the Yamaha to keep pumping out its high performance.

The angled stacks of the crowded stands, no more than a passing blur, gave way to a wide apron of tarmac which fronted a line of low, open workshops; the Donington pits. A fast and flickering impression of the mechanics and managers who waited with stopwatches for their riders to come whipping and roaring past, the information boards and the racers' girls in team livery, and then Freeman was leaning into the next corner, shifting his weight across the Yamaha's narrow seat to achieve the best balance. McBride was just inches from his rear wheel.

Simon Addison was still rocking in disbelief, as his hearing slowly returned. He still couldn't believe the physical force of the wall of noise that washed across the pits, as the leading group became a passing thunder, each machine a separate generator of raw power and each rider a distinct competitor for a moment, before merging back into the pack. It had been too long since he'd covered a race, Addison thought, as the cheering of the distant crowds and the tannoy echo of the track commentary became audible. Five years away from the sports pages, and he'd almost forgotten the electric tension; the excitement of the noise and the jostling and the pungent smell of burning oil. He'd first been aware of the stirring of old feelings, as he'd approached the entrance to the course down a solid avenue of glittering bikes. Innumerable machines stacked side-by-side, in a dense phalanx of oil, grease and metal, and topped with a rippling sea of mirrors; he'd read off some of the names as he'd walked along: Jawa, Suzuki, Triumph, Honda, Yamaha. Their forms were as varied as the names; solid, unassuming road bikes, ornate custom jobs which were probably hurried into a garage at the first sign of bad weather, bulky fibreglassed machines that emulated in shape, and some of their performances, the racers on the track. Why, he wondered with a sense of poignant regret, did he ever sell his old BSA and buy a car?

Addison squeezed through the crowd in search of the Trans-World bay. He wanted to get himself into the best possible position to see McBride coast victorious from the track. He was lying second to an unknown but that couldn't last, not with only four laps gone and the bulk of the race still ahead. Little more than a minute had passed, and the bikes were pounding down the straight again; a noticeable gap separated most of the riders, as they were shaken into order of speed and ability. Freeman and McBride were up front together, with a good three or four second lead over the five-man group that followed them. The whole crowd swivelled to follow, as one of the competitors peeled away and braked onto the tarmac apron, forced to concede the failure of his machine. His engine cut out suddenly as he left the main track, and he had to roll the last few yards to where his mechanics were running to meet him. He was shaking his head as he dismounted, and he walked away from the bike without looking back when the overalled men had taken its weight from him. A couple of journalists moved in, but Addison hung back; he'd seen somebody in Trans-World livery, and he moved to follow.

Ted Langley was on the grass. He'd been in the middle of the field and had found himself firmly trapped behind

Clarke Nichols of the Trans-World team. Langley had tried to cut through on the bend, but Nichols had blocked him; before he'd had chance to correct he was off the hard standing, and fighting to stay upright as the other riders zipped past. He hadn't fallen, but by the time he got back onto the track he'd lost both speed and time, and he scrubbed off some tyre by accelerating too hard to get back into the race. But his determination would be of little use to him, he was too far behind.

Trans-World probably had the most comprehensive and well equipped operation in the pits, as Addison could see when Langley roared away down the track alone. A brace of mechanics – Freeman and McBride throttling past, with still no change of position – stood ready to service the team's three Suzukis, and they wore well-cut red coveralls that were in sharp contrast to the oily fatigues that were to be seen elsewhere in the area. Spanners, gauges, wrenches and spares were laid out ready to be grabbed and used at seconds' notice; so many that it seemed that the crew might, with a few minutes' grace, feasibly assemble a complete new bike with the materials to hand. Not that this would do much good in mid-race, where the difference between winning and losing could be marked out in fractions of a second; those who like the unfortunate Langley were at the back of the field, knew that barring some impossible fluke, they were out of the serious competition.

Freeman had been holding on for longer than mere luck seemed to justify. Addison knew the name, but no more – except that he was a self-supporting, no-hope privateer. Now the race was moving towards its decisive closing laps, and Freeman was still there with a fierce grip on the lead. McBride was undoubtedly trying his hardest; he always pushed himself to his limits no matter how unimportant the competition might be in business terms, but it seemed that there was a real risk of his being beaten by an unknown, and an un-rated unknown at that. Addison looked around, wondering where Nick Freeman's backup might be.

The crowds across in the stands were shouting and cheering, their loyalties divided but no less enthusiastic. Many of them were fans and followers of McBride but equal numbers, it seemed, were rooting for the underdog, but that would only continue as long as he was winning. If McBride managed to pass him, Freeman would be assured of an instant slide back into obscurity.

A growing thunder from the far bend heralded the approach of the pack. Addison looked expectantly, then his attention was caught by a girl who stood a little apart from the rest. She was wearing a Trans-World team jacket, and pushing a cascade of long hair from her eyes as she gazed anxiously along the track.

Addison had seen her before somewhere, and he searched his memory for a moment before placing her. Julie something or other, he recalled, not actually McBride's girlfriend, more a friend of the team from way back. He'd seen her in magazines and on news broadcasts, often there when McBride cracked open the champagne after a win, never saying much.

Here they came, the mild summer sun glittering on the brightwork of the bikes as they swung around the bend and accelerated; the shouts of the crowds around the track became louder and even began to match the blanket roar of the cycles. At first it seemed that a single leader had emerged, but it was Langley, fallen so far back in the field that he was about to be lapped. Freeman and McBride were still together behind him, and then Addison saw what was causing such a loud response from the stands; McBride couldn't dodge through any gap in Freeman's placing on the corners, so he had drawn level on the *outside* of the bend and was using the superior power of his machine to make up the speed that he would normally lose. They came out even into the straight, but now Ted Langley blocked their way.

Langley was aware of their closeness, and risked a quick glance over his shoulder; his machine actually wobbled a little as his alarm was communicated through his body, for a touch of wheels at these speeds would be disastrous for all three riders. With a burst of throttle he drifted right out of line, opening up a gap wide enough to enable both of the leaders to pass through, without either giving way. The manoeuvre cost him some speed, but the loss was academic. Freeman and McBride rammed through the opening with their leading wheels level, and as they cleared his machine, Langley began to lean into his position for the next curve.

There was insufficient room – not enough distance left for him to get into a safe line for the bend. Even at this reduced speed he was too far out and would either spin off, or else lean too far in compensation, and get into a sideways slide. Desperately he braked, and the scream of pads and abrading rubber was being carried back to the pits, even over the passing roar of the four riders who were vying for third place.

It was difficult to see how, but Langley and his machine parted company; the bike showering sparks as its frame rasped and dragged across the tarmac surface. Langley was sliding as well, helmet clattering along the ground like a booted can, as he tumbled towards the grass verge and the crash barrier. The first rider behind him pulled his weight back in the saddle, and actually managed to lift his machine clear of Langley's bike as it scythed across his path, spinning free, and flying for a moment, before landing hard on the tarmac and accelerating away.

The rest of the field was passing now, stringing out into single file and moving between Langley's still form on the outside of the curve and the wreck of his bike on the inside. Marshals were running to the scene, and somewhere a siren was sounding; several people had broken with safety regulations and were running along the track itself. Langley lifted a hand, dropped it again, was still. It seemed like disaster, terrible carnage; but already the attention of the pits, if not of the stands, was returning to the race. The track was being cleared and a stretcher was being rushed over, and now the concerns and preoccupations of those around Addison were returning to their own rider, their own team.

Five years of light features and society froth fell away from Addison as if they'd never happened. This was where he belonged, and this was the kind of coverage he wanted to go on writing; his shirt was damp and sticking to his back, and not because of the mild summer sun. It was the shared tension of the pits, the sympathetic agony of hard competition where lives were on the line; the smell of the oil, the wide open track and the dense excitement of the yelling crowds.

The two riders were level as they disappeared from sight, and in spite of McBride's expertise and quality backup, there was still a slim chance that the race might, in the end, belong to Nick Freeman. Addison was still near the girl, the obvious place to be when McBride pulled in to pose for his victory photographs, but now he looked around uneasily for Nick Freeman's outfit.

The girl moved aside, reaching behind her for a half-emptied can of Coke. Beyond her, and now in Addison's line of sight, was a tall young black. He was wearing dark overalls and a shapeless woollen cap, but he had the kind of easy elegance that would enhance any clothing; in short, he had style. He was holding the obligatory stopwatch and was looking up the track as the field came around for the last lap. It seemed impossible, but Bruce McBride and

Nick Freeman were still fighting level, one or the other starting to fall back, and then drawing up again with a fine correction.

Addison looked again at the young man with the watch. He was alone, seemingly not a part of the general pattern around him; nor was he in sponsored livery, heavy with garish advertising, and worn by most of the backup teams. Addison tried to edge towards him without looking conspicuous, tried to get a look at the name on the front of his jacket.

Nick Freeman. It was badly embroidered, about right for a nobody. The roar from the track was growing, voices and machines mixed as this last opportunity to turn failure into success began to slip by, but the hand with the stopwatch was steady with a languid calm that suggested easy self-control.

Out on the track, some distance from the pits and the flag, McBride and Freeman were leaning into a sharp curve. Freeman could see out of the corner of his eye that McBride was giving him a quick sideways glance, but he refused to allow his attention to be distracted for even a fraction of a second; 'I'm holding you off, you bastard,' he thought, 'you're trying like *hell* and you can't pass me, how do you like *that*, Mister Bruce bloody McBride?'

McBride was easing forward. Freeman gunned the throttle to draw up and cancel the move. Nothing happened. McBride was still moving ahead, and as Freeman twisted the throttle grip he felt an appalling surge of impotence as the bike failed to respond; McBride was ahead and clear now but Freeman was still falling back, his motor starting to splutter and complain as the Yamaha gave up its efforts. McBride threw a fast look over his shoulder, and it seemed that he was grinning behind his visor as he pulled away alone. Smoke was starting to feather from the Yamaha, and Freeman straightened slightly, pulling the bike away onto the outside of the track as a close bunch of the other riders flashed past him on the inside.

'Are you Nick Freeman's manager?' Addison asked the young black as the chequered flag was being raised in anticipation of the leader's appearance on the home straight.

Eyes moved from the track, gave Addison the briefest glance, moved back again. Then a short, barely perceptible shake of the head. The first of the group was around the curve and in sight, a single rider with nobody pressing him. The chequered flag was up, ready to sweep down for the winner.

'His mechanic, then?'

McBride was throttling back and had a hand in the air even before he had passed under the flag. He had a clear nine seconds' lead on the next man across the line, who wasn't Freeman. Nor was the next. There was applause and general congratulations in the Trans-World camp, and the start of a move towards the pits, as McBride swung across and made for the apron.

'You're Nick Freeman's mechanic?'

Cider Jones again turned his brown eyes to Simon Addison, and gave him an alligator-wide smile. 'Well, I was when I came in,' he said, 'but I ain't so sure now.' And he pocketed his still-running stopwatch as he moved away, giving Addison a bright little wave as he went.

TWO

It had been the last race of the meeting, so nobody objected when Cider Jones, black and bouncy strolled out onto the track and began to walk down the course. Most of the attention was on McBride anyway, as he rolled into the Trans-World enclosure, hopping from his bike to the steps of his trailer and exchanging his stars-and-stripes helmet for the inevitable champagne and garland. The champagne had been well-shaken and it erupted out over the swelling crowd of journalists, photographers and autograph-seekers; the garland he jammed over the head of a journalist who had once reported him to have bedded every presentable girl on the racing circuit. *Smut of the Year*, McBride crowned him, to the delight of the crowd, and when the reporter indicated Julie and said, 'What's *her* name?' McBride told him 'Bugs Bunny'.

What's it like being Number Four in the world, somebody else asked. McBride said it was like being number four hundred and what sort of question was *that*? There seemed to be a genuine antagonism somewhere under the banter, an unspoken resentment of someone who won, and won as often and as ostentatiously as Bruce McBride. He knew it, and he played to it.

Elsewhere in the pits riders were removing their helmets, becoming human beings again instead of the anonymous, battle-ready gladiators who competed on the track. McBride's two team-mates had released their machines to the care of the Trans-World mechanics and now they stood, easy and smiling on the fringe of the crowd, untroubled by the attention that was being lavished on the star of their circus. For the moment, they supported him;

eventually their turn would come. Other riders along the line were reacting to their own match performances in different ways; some obviously pleased at an increase in personal attainment that promised well for a later career, others critically probing the engines of their bikes as if the oil and rubber entrails could reveal the causes of their failure.

The Park's service wagon crossed in front of Cider, horn blaring as he skipped back and waved it past graciously. 'Smart-arse,' the driver called, and Cider grinned back as though acknowledging some kind of praise.

The truck moved across his sightline carrying the gathered wreckage and split fibreglass fairing of Langley's bike, Cider sighted Freeman for the first time. He was pushing his heavy machine, coming up level with the grandstand, his head down. Cider moved to meet him, and Freeman looked up as he approached. Nick's normally clear eyes were showing tiredness and depression, and his hair – unruly at the best of times – was plastered and limp from the constriction of his racing helmet.

'Anybody get hurt?' he said, and it sounded as if he were afraid of the answer.

Cider shrugged. 'Word is that Langley's got concussion, somebody else bust a collarbone. What about you?'

'Bloody rings. That's the third time, Cider.'

Cider gave his *well, man, that's life* nod, but Nick continued to stare in mute accusation. 'Hey,' Cider said. 'What's that mean?'

'I was right up there. I had McBride where he couldn't get past me. *McBride*, Cider. He was trying and he couldn't.'

'Not how it looks from here.'

'I told you, the bloody rings went again. All of a sudden I lost power and started burning oil, and that flash Yank was head-down for the flag while I was on the grass.'

Cider's eyes widened in exaggerated surprise. 'And you're blaming *me*?'

Freeman hesitated, just long enough to make the point. ' 'Course not,' he said.

'I worked all through the night on that bastard, Nick, and I know the way you ride. All you need is the smell of a win and you'll pour in everything you've got, now am I right or am I wrong?'

Freeman didn't seem to have heard. 'Regional finals in a week, as well.'

'Regional finals, nothing.'

That one got through. 'What do you mean?' Freeman said, slowing down and balancing the bike with difficulty. 'What are you talking about?'

'I mean there's no point going on with it. You want to win races, and this heap of shit just wants to fall apart and roll back to the junkyard where it belongs. Might as well face it, you can't argue with its instincts.'

There was some truth in what Cider was saying. Freeman's bike made a poor comparison with the likes of McBride's finely-tuned Suzuki. The fairing was hand-built and sanded, and the lettering on it was badly proportioned, whilst mechanically the bike was so full of adaptations and compromises that it could no longer be said to be of any specific or identifiable make.

Cider started to walk away, changed his mind and came back, kicked the bike, and started off again.

'Where are you going?' Freeman called after him, bewildered.

'Get the van,' Cider said, raising his voice but not turning. 'That's unless you *want* to sit in a twenty-mile line to get back into town.'

'Hey, Cider!' Nick shouted. 'Cider, come on!'

No reaction, Cider just walked on. Usually, apologies were irrelevant between them; Nick would rail and complain for a while, and Cider would let him get it out of his system and then bring him down with some deflating remark to get him laughing again. But this time looked like being different.

'Cider!' he shouted again, before distance and the light breeze could carry his voice away, 'I can't hold the bike up any more!'

Cider turned and looked back. The machine was starting to lean under its own weight, starting to win the battle against Freeman's race-tired body. Already the edge had gone from Cider's anger, and the situation was beginning to reassert itself as familiar; they had been disappointed before, but now the disappointment was intensified by the way in which it followed near-success. As Cider returned he was keenly aware of his own folly. He preferred not to speculate on whether the folly lay in the walking away or the going back.

'Carry on like that and you'll hurt her feelings,' Freeman said. 'Better tell her you love her.'

Cider gave him a smouldering look as he reached over and gripped the handlebars. As soon as he was holding the bike, Freeman let go and started to walk off, waving with elegant grace to the people who were emptying out of the stand on the other side of the trackside barrier. A few of them looked back, blankly.

'Nick!' Cider shouted, helpless with the weight of the bike, and Freeman glanced over his shoulder and grinned. 'Nick, one of these days I'm going to kill you!'

After a few yards he caught up, and Freeman took over his share of the load again. There was, he admitted to himself, a lot of truth in what Cider had said, determination and skill were not enough on their own, a rider needed first-class engineering under him to make the most of his abilities. Freeman, as a privateer, an independent without any resources other than his own income, could never hope to succeed. The only way would be for him to join someone else's team where he could expect to be instructed to set the pace, thin out the field, aim for a comfortable third. But he lived to race, and raced to win; he'd had enough of playing the subservient company game in the garage stores.

In one way it would have been better if Greg had come in on the team, but, longterm, it would never have worked out. For Freeman, a bike was an efficient means of winning a race, whilst for his brother it was an object in itself. Greg would never spend one night grinding down a set of oversized rings for a quick repair; he would measure and calculate, perhaps find some way of improving the design of the part, which in turn would suggest some complementary improvement. Any component that didn't win his satisfaction would be stripped down and rebuilt, and if this process revealed any flaw or inferiority, the part would be scrapped and the procedure begun again. In the end the bike would be perfect, but it would also be a month too late for the race.

Cider, although he didn't have Greg's inspiration, was a good racing mechanic. He was fast and efficient, and he could work magic in seemingly hopeless situations; magic, but not miracles. First-class engineering was expensive, and the costs of competition were high. The resources commanded by Cider and Nick were barely enough to keep the team on the tracks at its present level, let alone elevate it to greater success – and without the unofficial use of equipment at the garage they could have forgotten their hopes altogether.

They weren't looking forward to their arrival in the pits with the sick machine. Although nobody really paid them much attention as they came down the sliproad to the apron, their embarrassment hardly lessened. This was worse than coming in last, it was pure shame. But it had happened before and would probably happen again, and perhaps they ought to be getting used to it.

Most of the press had drifted away by now, and the fans and the followers had taken their place. McBride was signing books, programmes, scraps of paper – anything that was put in front of him with a quick and practised scrawl that only vaguely resembled his name.

'This one next, Bruce,' Julie said, lifting a boy who was too small to see over the others. McBride reached for his programme and made a couple more loops with the pen. Then he seemed to see something that he'd been looking for, and he moved away from the trailer. The crowd moved with him, more books and programmes held out.

'Here's a guy whose autograph you should be getting,' he said, picking a book out of the air and holding it out with a pen to Nick Freeman. Nick looked around, embarrassed by the sudden attention and hampered by the weight of the Yamaha. 'This guy's a good rider,' McBride went on. 'Be really good someday.' He scribbled on the book himself when Nick didn't take it, and passed it back to a waiting hand.

'Bruce McBride,' he said, as a superfluous introduction to Nick. He was slightly taller than Freeman, fair-haired and suntanned, his teeth even and California-white. Freeman was suddenly aware of his own unkempt appearance, his old worn leathers, his unimpressive machine. Beyond McBride he could see that the girl was watching them. 'Listen,' McBride went on, 'when the guy up front's in trouble, you have to give him room.'

Cider resisted the temptation to close his eyes and pray. Here's Bruce McBride, the world-famous racing star, and he's just going to hand down a few words of wisdom to the no-account charity case, that he's just beaten into the ground. From somewhere came the sound of a couple of camera shutters, which didn't help.

'You'll need to hold off a little on those sharp curves. That guy . . . what was his name?'

'Ted Langley,' someone supplied.

'That guy Langley got a concussion, but it could have been a lot worse. So just ease off a little here and there, won't you?' The smile broadened. 'Ride with you again some day. Take care.'

He patted Nick's arm and started to turn away. 'Forget it, Nick,' thought Cider, 'you'll only make yourself look bad.'

'Wait a minute,' said Freeman. McBride turned, still amiable. 'I was on the inside.' Nick went on. 'Why didn't *you* drop back?'

McBride, with the polite tolerance that only a winner can afford, said, 'Because I was leading.'

'We were dead level. There wasn't an inch in it.'

'Hey, now – I was holding back because of your position. Just remember: don't try to hold on when you haven't got the speed – not when it means putting another rider in danger.'

'Crap,' said Freeman. 'I was on the inside and you wouldn't fall back. Langley gave me room to come through and you pushed right through the middle. He didn't have any chance of getting back into line for the next curve.'

'Listen . . . Freeman,' McBride said, reading the name off the leathers, 'if anybody's out of line right now it's you. And unless you've been riding under another name these last five years' – here he glanced around, seeking and receiving the tacit approval of the crowd – 'I'd say you're out of your class as well.'

'I'll remember. When the great man comes slumming, the rest of us had better keep out of his way,' Freeman sneered.

At that moment, McBride's manager pushed between them and McBride reluctantly withdrew. With a wave of his hand he turned away; Freeman was obviously such a jumped-up microbe, that he merited no further attention. The girl looked for a moment, then followed.

'It's bad enough feeling like a piece of shit pushing the damn bike home,' Cider complained in a low voice. 'What do you have to go and start something like that for?'

'It's true. He couldn't pass me, so he sat on me. That's what forced Ted Langley to move out so far.'

'So what? You'd have a hard time proving it wasn't legal.'

'Stuff whether it was legal, it wasn't fair.'

'Am I hearing right? Where did you get the dumb-shit idea that you had a right to expect things to be *fair* in this crummy business?'

'Thanks, Cider. Your confidence sustains me in times of trouble.'

Cider made a helpless gesture, and the yellow Yamaha lurched alarmingly before he could get his hands back on the frame.

'Look at this,' he said. Freeman looked; he didn't have much choice as the massive bike transporter in brilliant Trans-World livery turned into the pits and drew past them, guided by the signals of mechanics in spotless team colours. 'You play the game their way, that's the kind of backup you get.'

Nick nodded. 'I'd give a lot for an outfit like that.'

Cider was about to go on but stopped abruptly, surprised at his easy victory. He looked at Freeman, and then looked in the direction that his eyes were fixed. 'No,' he said after a moment. 'You don't want an outfit like that.'

'Why not?'

'The hips are too wide, waist too small . . .'

Freeman took his eyes off the girl, where they'd been for the last few seconds.

'You sending me up?' he said suspiciously.

26

'Right, I'm sending you up.'

'Bastard!'

Freeman drew back an exaggerated fist, and Cider made an exaggerated feint. The Yamaha teetered for a moment with nobody holding it before it keeled unceremoniously over, crashing to the ground between them. For a few seconds it rattled in a way that no functioning machine ever should.

'Why don't we get *very* drunk?' Nick said, as if he'd suddenly discovered the answer to all their problems.

'Because we haven't got any money,' Cider said. Voicing the one problem that Nick hadn't considered. They bent to lift the bike.

'Hi, Nick,' said a voice. Freeman looked up to see Stoddard, another independent rider who was marginally less destitute than himself. He wore tiny pebble glasses with lenses like the bottoms of Coke bottles; it was a standing joke between them that Nick would go over to him on the grid before a race and carefully point out the direction in which the bikes would be going. Stoddard helped them with the Yamaha and said, 'What happened?'

Cider cut in before Nick could answer.

'You ever hear this guy boasting that a race would be so easy he could walk it?'

'Go on, Cider,' Stoddard said. 'That's how Nick finishes all his races.'

THREE

It was nearly midnight when the old Ford van pulled into the wide North London street. Here it was quiet but never completely dead; the rooms above and behind the shops were now given over to cheap rooms with failing plumbing, whose tenants kept no regular hours. It was cosmopolitan and vital, or it was a deadly and depressing urban jungle, depending on the disposition of the observer.

Some of the more vulnerable ground-floor windows were covered with sheets of plywood; pasted haphazardly with handbills. Rock concerts, unknown pub-bands, pregnancy advice, and the enigmatic religious message; within a day they were all torn across, and fresh notices, equally unauthorized, were added.

As usual, the slow progress through London's faltering traffic system had taken almost as long as the straight drive down the motorway – almost, but not quite, since the van was in slightly worse mechanical condition than the bike it usually carried. Cider, by repeated questioning while Freeman was trapped in the passenger seat, had finally drawn from Nick the admission that, well, *perhaps* he might have pushed the revs up too high on the practice lap and *perhaps* this had something to do with the failure of the machine later in the race . . .

Cider hadn't been very pleased. He thought of the work involved: another sleepless night working on cheap parts with inadequate tools, all to be blown and burnt for nothing more crucial than a practice lap.

'So I won't do it again,' Freeman said. 'I'll even write you out a statement and sign it.'

'I know. It was to impress that dumb girl.'

'What girl?'

'You know damn well what girl. The one you wouldn't take your eyes off every time she walked through the pits.'

'Oh, *that* girl.'

'You've already got a girl, Nick. You should be looking at mechanics.'

'I don't need another mechanic.'

'You do after today. I got better things to do with my time.'

'Come on, Cider,' Nick said, 'we've got the regional finals next week.'

Cider pulled out to pass a lorry, found he didn't have the speed, and dropped back. 'I'll read about it in the papers,' he said.

'Why are you starting this again?'

'I'm not starting anything, I'm finishing something. You'll never make it on that heap of scrap we've got behind us, and I'm sick of roping it together, and patching it up time after time and pretending that you will.'

'We'll fix it up, Cider. They won't know what's hit 'em.'

'Sure we will. We'll use oversized rings and secondhand chains . . . pardon me, that was my mistake, we used all the top-class spares up last week. Now we're down to cornflake boxes and pieces of string. Won't know what hit 'em? Ride that thing once more and bits of it will be hitting *everybody*!'

'You'd never make a rider,' Freeman said as he settled back in his seat. 'Too emotional.' Cider made strangled noises of frustration, and tightened his grip on the wheel in a way that suggested he wished it was Freeman's neck.

The van wheezed to a halt outside Nick's shabby hut. He climbed out and then turned to gather his helmet and leathers from the seat. Cider looked across at him; he could manage a pretty cool look of weary disapproval when he worked on it. In the back of the van the maligned bike stood, bulky in the soft rimlit glow of reflected streetlights. Tired as he was, Freeman grinned.

'See you on Monday,' he said, 'and don't worry about the rings . . . I think I know where I can get you some good ones, cheap.' He closed the door quickly, before Cider could get in with a reply. 'Take care,' he said, slapping the coachwork and giving a little wave before turning to cross the street to his front door.

'Hey!' Cider shouted, 'Who said I'm going to fit new rings? Who said that?'

Freeman waved again, knowing better than to reply, as Cider let in the noisy clutch and moved off.

It was hardly a street for a champion to live on, but the prospect of escape was certainly an incentive to success. This wasn't where Freeman belonged, and he knew it; he also knew that, without his racing, this was where he would stay. Cider understood, and, to an extent, he agreed. He would come around.

As he dug in his pocket for his key, Freeman wondered idly what kind of background McBride had. Probably sunshine and money, and a steady supply of admiring girls. Top guy in his yearbook, or whatever the system was in American high schools, where they made a fuss over the top creep and gave everybody else a complex that would take them ten years or more to dispel. One day he would go over there, when he was rich and a racing star and didn't have to worry about details like scraping the money together for a ticket. He'd ride from coast to coast, taking his time and perhaps doing guest spots at tracks along the way; not worrying about a schedule or the dismal beckoning of his job in the garage stores.

It was a pleasant daydream, but Nick didn't often waste much energy on such speculation. He opened the door quietly – their rooms were near the stairs, and Carol had probably been disturbed enough by late arrivals already. He reached inside for the hall light.

It was a spring-button affair, one which gave a measured dose of light and then popped out to leave you in darkness. The switch was worn and the period was short, so that anybody above the first floor had to dash up the stairs and get to the next switch in the circuit before the blackness returned. In the pale yellow glow of the cheap shade, Freeman could see enough to avoid the bicycle and the baby-carriage that seemed to be permanent features of the hallway. He stepped around them and closed the door, moving towards the angled staircase which led to what the Italian landlord called the 'studio apartment' – one bedroom and a reasonably large sitting room with an overhead skylight and a partitioned-off area for the kitchen.

The switch clicked and the hall lights went out just as he was letting himself into the flat, but he could see pretty well by the streetlights and the flashing signs outside the window. He perceived a movement in the shadows near the bedroom door.

'Carol?' he whispered.

'Nick,' Carol said, 'where have you been?' As she came forward he could see her face; she seemed weary, and her eyes were reddened with crying. 'I thought you'd never get here.'

He glanced at his watch, awkward with the leathers, but the glow from the dial was too faint to make out. 'What's the matter,' he said. 'Why aren't you in bed?'

'Keep your voice down,' she said. Suddenly her voice became gentle and sad. 'Tina's here. Greg's been killed.'

She waited as he absorbed the information. From the bedroom he could now hear the sounds of sobbing, but they were hollow and unreal, as distant and incomprehensible as the night itself had suddenly become. Nick tried to ask how. He framed the question, but nothing came out.

Carol told him anyway; about the trail bikes and the chalk pits – Nick remembered them, he'd done some fun riding there on his first bike – and about the accident, and how there was nothing that could have been done because Greg was dead before the ambulance arrived.

She watched him as he took in the details, sympathizing with his misery and adding it to her own. It was only when Carol had gone to check on Tina, and Nick was left alone in the sitting room, he found his first words.

'Oh, shit,' he said.

FOUR

It was late Monday morning when Julie Prince arrived at the hotel in Chelsea which was Trans-World's London base for the season. A uniformed doorman bowed her in, making her feel a little embarrassed, as always, and as the tinted plate door closed behind her she looked around the lobby, with its mirrors and palms, to see if there was anyone she knew. There were people with bags moving out, other people with bags moving in, a number of Japanese tourists sitting on and around the low seats amongst expensive plants, but nobody from Trans-World. As she crossed the carpeted floor to where the lobby opened out into the elevator bay, a Pan Am crew were emerging, swinging their light luggage easily as they strolled out towards a waiting bus.

Trans-World had taken over most of the top floor of the building. It was the penthouse level, luxurious by anybody's standards. When she stepped out of the elevator Danny came forward to meet her, glancing inside to make sure nobody was there who shouldn't be. He was big and broad, an ex-policeman who would make any suit look overstretched, and he sat on a hard chair just out of line with the sliding doors. There was always somebody on the chair, one of a team of three security men, all imposing in size and power, all surprisingly gentle in speech and manner. Trans-World took no chances with its property.

'Find what you were after, miss?' Danny asked as he escorted her to McBride's suite.

'I looked at a couple of places, and saw one I liked. There isn't much on the market right now, it seems.'

33

'Never is in London, miss. Not at prices anyone can afford – unless you've got an oil well, that is.'

'Unfortunately, I haven't, but I've got to be somewhere within reach of St. Thomas's before the semester begins. Besides which, it gets pretty tiring tagging along with the racing team all the time.'

'I wouldn't have thought you'd have minded that,' Danny said, and tapped on the door to McBride's suite. There was a muffled call from within, and Danny produced a passkey. 'I've heard say you're keen on the racing. Not like some of the others.'

'Why, Danny, do I sense a note of cynicism buried somewhere in there?'

'Me? Never. But I've seen them all, the gold-diggers and the good-time girls. You're all right.'

He held the door open as she stepped through, his eyes on the corridor behind him to ensure that his vigil was uninterrupted. She smiled and thanked him, and meant it.

There was another of the security team inside the door, just for good measure. The french windows were open onto the roof garden, and McBride was out there in a towelling bathrobe, his hair damp and ruffled from the shower; over the distant sounds of London traffic Julie could hear the hard-edged voice of team manager Al Peterson.

'You can't fly back from Holland on the same night,' he was insisting, 'because if the flight gets delayed—'

'I can sleep on the plane,' McBride cut in, as if the solution was so obvious that he couldn't understand how Peterson could have missed it.

'You sleep on the plane and what do you think you'll feel like?'

'I'll feel okay.' McBride was obviously baiting Peterson, delighting in his exasperation.

'You'll feel like a bag of warm crap.'

'All right, then I'll call you up and you can bring me one.'

'Am I interrupting?' Julie said as they came in from the roof garden. McBride immediately went into his dying-man act, clutching his heart and staggering about the room, whilst Peterson and Julie looked on and laughed.

Part of the suite was cluttered with the detritus of success; airline timetables, rumpled year-planning charts with broken lines in different colours drawn in, a stack of McBride photographs waiting for signature that had somehow been pushed over and spread around. In the next room the bed was still unmade, and the two trays with unfinished breakfasts had been pushed to one side: a bitten croissant, two glasses, sticky with juice, a cold coffee jug.

'Julie,' Peterson said, sweeping over to her with his arms outstretched, 'you came just in time to save my life. Will you talk to this idiot?'

'I'll talk to idiots, but I'm not making any guarantees of success. What's the problem?'

McBride had levered himself off the floor, where it seemed he was getting insufficient sympathy. 'It's Al's blood pressure,' he said. 'He can't cope with the slightest strain, so he wants me to live in a padded box between races.'

'A padded box?' Peterson said. 'What he needs is a padded *cell*. You want to check blood pressure? Have a look at his. I don't think there's any getting through to his brain.'

'Please,' Julie protested, 'lay off with the medical terms. I'm going to get enough of them after the start of semester at St Thomas's.'

'You've found yourself somewhere to stay, like you wanted?' Peterson asked.

'Sure have. A sort of apartment.'

'Sort of?' said McBride. 'Can I see it?'

35

'Only with a microscope.'

Peterson said, 'If you want to move in with the team, Julie, the invitation still stands. Until you get fixed up with something you really want, that is.'

'Oh no,' said McBride, 'this is one independent lady. I tried all the lines and she doesn't fall for any of them.'

'There you go, schmucko,' Peterson said as he took Julie by the arm, and guided her to one of the none-too-comfortable chairs, 'you finally met someone who doesn't fall for the big hero and superstar routine. And don't it tear you up?'

'Banging my head on a wall. But then, she's seen it all before.'

There was a momentary silence that could have been embarrassment, and then McBride went on, talking quickly as if to cover up with a change of subject. 'Listen,' he said, 'why don't you come with me to Holland on Friday?'

'Holland? I thought you were supposed to be racing at Brand's Hatch on Saturday.'

'That's what everybody says,' Peterson interrupted, 'except him.'

'Come on, Al. It's an easy turnaround.'

'What does that matter?' Peterson turned to Julie. 'He's running number four in the world and he wants to ride three races in one week. I tell him twenty times and he still won't listen. You want to try?'

'You can't ride three races in one week,' Julie said, attempting to be serious and almost managing.

'You hear that?' said Peterson.

McBride looked dubious. 'It might sound better over lunch. I don't hear so well when I'm hungry.'

'Aren't you dieting?' Julie said, and Peterson burst out into a triumphant and mocking laugh. Obviously she had raised, without prompting, an earlier topic of contention.

36

'I'm skin and bone under this shirt, doctor,' Peterson said, wide-eyed and mock-solemn. 'What say we get rid of the old man, and you can give me an examination?'

It was almost eleven when Freeman finally arrived at the garage, crossing the tidy forecourt which was the showroom side of the operation, and turning into the complex of less attractive buildings that lay back from the main road. The folding doors of the service bays were all opened in deference to the season, and the slick, empty music of a commercial radio station was playing somewhere on a cheap transistor, battling against the hammering of the pressure drills and the loud clangs of falling metal. Most of the bays had vehicles jacked high on their hydraulic lifts, cars with their wheels hanging like the limbs of suspended tortoises; the mechanics worked beneath, strange puppeteers, oily to the elbows.

Cider Jones was levering a ruptured tyre from its rims, when he saw Nick passing through. The persona of the weekend racer sat uneasily within the role of the stores clerk, and Freeman rarely showed much enthusiasm for the dull and meticulous prison that reached out to embrace him every Monday; but today he was really down, and even at this distance it showed.

As Freeman walked towards the half-glassed door to the stores, head bowed and his jacket slung across his shoulder, Cider moved to meet him.

'Nice to see you this afternoon, Mister Freeman,' he said, laying on heavy with the irony, and a couple of the nearer mechanics looked up and smiled. 'May I be the first to say how pleased we all are that you could get here today and spare us a moment of your valuable time?'

Nick attempted to go through into the stores, but Cider wasn't going to let him get away so easily.

'You any idea what *time* this is? Ol' Wiggins is blowing his stack in there. Better just run outside and break a few limbs or something, 'cause that's the only way you're going to impress him. And *then* he'll want copies of the X-rays for the front office. Even *you've* never been this late before.'

'I never arranged a funeral before,' Nick said, and pushed through into the stores.

Cider was left outside for a few seconds, his mouth hanging open, lost for a snappy answer. He caught the door as it swung towards him and followed through; Freeman had thrown his jacket onto a hook and was pulling on a tattered white storeman's coat.

'Hey, Nick,' Cider said with real concern, 'what's wrong, man?'

'My brother killed himself Saturday,' Nick said quietly.

He wasn't ready to talk, so Cider left him alone for a while. After a couple of minutes word had reached Wiggins of Freeman's arrival. The garage Foreman was a pleasant enough individual in his forties, but a working lifetime of invoices, timesheets and holiday chits had drained most of the imagination and personality out of him. His office was a breeze-block annexe at the end of the service bays, where he had an old painted desk, a cracked telephone and a couple of giveaway girlie calendars on the bare wall which featured, what were generally agreed to be, the ugliest models ever photographed. It was from here that he emerged and marched determinedly towards the stores.

He was out again within two minutes, all his threats and reproofs deflated before they had been expressed. Cider was tempted to smile, but he suppressed this with a swift dose of guilt; after all, he'd *known* Greg, admittedly not very well, but there was a strange and disturbing sensation when he contemplated the life-line that had been so abruptly cut. A little shift had occurred in the world, all the constants and assumptions of life taking a slightly new shading to their meaning. Like all change it carried the capacity to frighten, and the mind sought escape. No evasion, though, for Nick Freeman.

Lunch hour came around, and Cider did his usual trick of slipping out ten minutes early, to beat the mid-day rush at the pseudo-American grill, which was the nearest accessible carry-out. It was called *Elmer's Place*, and the choice ranged from boxed chicken bones in batter with a plastic cup of cold beans, to thin rubbery burgers on stale bread with an optional slice of yellow wax. The 'service' was by a taciturn Iranian who wrapped and delivered the junk food with not even a suspicion of a smile.

Everybody else was drifting out as Cider arrived back at the garage, but there was no sign of Nick. Encumbered by a large paper bag and a couple of cans, he turned and pushed open the sprung door to the stores by leaning back on it. As he passed through, he could hear Nick on the telephone at the far end of the room. Cider walked down one of the long avenues of grey Dexion shelving that was stacked with motor spares; it was like a supermarket from an enigmatic dream, dull and unappealing with goods fit only for robot customers.

Nick was trying not to argue with a trade client, but he was barely succeeding. There was an order form in front of him and he seemed to be making notes, but as Cider dumped the bag and the Cokes on the low desk he noticed that Nick was only doodling, his hand working aimlessly and independently of his mind.

Cider pulled up an old chair and used the heel of his elegant boot to hook out a filing-cabinet drawer as a footrest, and waited for Nick to finish.

'May I recommend the house wine?' he said as he emptied four tinfoil shapes out of the bag. 'It's fully-bodied

39

with a delicate aroma and a light touch on the palate that doesn't fuck up the flavour of your cheeseburger.'

Freeman pushed the order pad aside and reached for the can, twisting off the ring-pull without comment. He unwrapped one of the burgers and looked at it without enthusiasm.

'What's this?' he said. 'Bike-burger? That's what Greg was. Bike-burger.'

'Knock it off, Nick.'

Cider waited for a while, uncertain of what to say next. He knew it wasn't the time to be hip, but for friendship's sake he couldn't let the silence go on for ever.

'How's Tina making out?' he asked. Nick started to speak, but then shrugged helplessly, so Cider went on. 'What's she going to do for money?'

'Don't know, yet. Sell the house, I suppose. Anyway there's money on her side of the family, not like ours. Greg was the only one who was really making it anywhere, with the degree and the good job and everything. Tina doesn't think he was insured.'

'That's bad.'

'It was so early, the last thing you'd think of. He was only thirty . . .' Nick did a fast calculation – 'thirty-two.'

'Like they tell you in the ads. You never see it coming.'

'There's something else, as well. Tina's pregnant.'

This was a problem of the living, something that Cider could readily understand. He shook his head. 'Poor kid,' he said. 'Is she going to sell his bikes?'

Nick frowned. 'It wasn't exactly the best time to ask her.'

'But you're going to?' Cider persisted, a knowing tone coming into his voice as he began to get the measure of Nick's thoughts.

Nick seemed to be shocked at the suggestion. 'Who says I'm going to?'

40

'Nobody has to say it.'

Even Cider was surprised at the way Nick's obsession lay so close to the surface, even at a time like this.

'What about his race bike? You going to tell me that you're not even interested to see how far on he got from those first drawings he showed you?'

'They were only drawings.'

'Sure, and they had you squirming with envy even then. Please, Nick, do yourself a favour and forget the idea.'

'You brought it up. Are you trying to make out I'm pleased Greg's dead, or something?'

'I'm trying to say that one death in the family's enough. That was always your trouble, you get the chance and then you blast away without control. I can't sling you into the back of the van and then start looking around for spares to get you going again.'

The telephone rang, so unexpectedly that the handset seemed to jump and rattle in surprise. Nick grabbed it, more in relief than irritation, listening for a moment to what sounded to Cider a couple of feet away like somebody gargling.

He made a couple of placatory noises and then said, 'We'll move it. We were just on our way when you rang. If you hadn't called, it would have gone by now.'

There was some more gargling, then Nick hung up.

'Wiggy wants the bike moved,' he said.

The Ford van, still with the ailing race bike strapped inside, was parked amongst the firm's vehicles, by the side of the service building. The concrete had been painted with yellow parking lines, but these were invariably ignored, as were the hand-lettered plaques which indicated spaces reserved for the management. But they preferred not to risk leaving their Volvos and Rovers in an area through which stricken vehicles were shunted to and from the service bays, choosing instead to send out an office boy, with a bag of coins, to feed their various parking meters.

The van was an eyesore, sitting there amongst the resprays, and the warranty cars and the new vehicles prepared for delivery. Little wonder that Wiggins wanted it moved before a complaint was made. There was a padlock fitted across the double doors at the back, an adaptation made by some earlier owner for greater security; Nick wrestled with the stiff tumblers to get it open, before swinging aside the doors and reaching in for the bike ramp.

'It'll be out of your league,' Cider said as Nick climbed inside and unhooked the cables which held the yellow bike. 'However much of it he got finished, you wouldn't be able to handle it.'

'I know,' said Nick, but Cider was unconvinced.

'You just won't see it, will you?'

'Nothing to see,' said Nick. He kicked the blocks away from the bike's wheels with more force than was necessary, and heaved to guide it towards the ramp.

'You're the most stubborn bastard I ever met.' Cider reached up and took the weight of the machine as it began to roll.

There was a small storeroom at the back of the spares depot which Nick, using the freedom granted to him as stores clerk, had set aside to garage the machine. Nobody above Wiggins knew this, and Wiggins, as long as nobody from above was on his back, was sufficiently free of spite and perversity to make no objection of his own.

He came out at the sound of their raised voices, wearing a white coat that was regularly laundered and pressed by his wife as a supportive effort to his slow climb towards middle-management. 'Hey, you two!' he said, 'You're past the lunch break and into the firm's time. All right?'

'We're putting it away,' Nick assured him.

'What, in the stockroom?' Wiggins said anxiously.

'Don't worry, I'll keep it quiet.'

'Why don't you keep it at home, instead?'

'The landlord doesn't like me getting oil on his carpets. Don't worry about it.'

Wiggins glanced around, wary of any early returnees from expense-account lunches. 'If the front office sees you,' he said, 'you know who'll get fired, don't you?'

'Don't get steamed up, Wiggy,' Cider cut in, 'nobody wants to put your job on the line. Anybody gets fired, it'll be this idiot here. That's if he doesn't realize his big dream and get wiped out on some circuit somewhere.' He let go of the bike and made a brief gesture of disgust. 'I don't know why I waste my time,' he said, and walked off shaking his head.

Wiggins moved after him quickly. 'Cider,' he said as he caught up in the doorway, 'there's something you ought to know before you go around shooting your mouth off. Nick's brother died at the weekend, so lay off him, will you?'

'Listen, man, I know about his brother. So lay off me, okay?'

'Give us a hand, Wiggy,' Nick called, and Wiggins turned and reached obediently for the bike without thinking.

In the service bay, the layout was pretty much as before. Some of the cars were different, some of the ramps that had been up were down, but the same cheerless and utilitarian atmosphere prevailed. The transistor radio was somewhere near, still pumping out pop music and chatto, and as Cider walked along to his own bay he could hear the filtered jigging of some white man's reggae. 'Jesus,' he thought, glad to find some other target onto which he could direct his annoyance, 'it's nearly enough to make you racist.'

The music got louder as he moved around an immobilized Saab. Somebody was underneath, working from a sliding trolley; the sour-faced and belligerent Jack Davis, Cider could tell from the man's shoes. The radio was propped on the car's rear fender, the dismantled parts of the oil sump spread on the ground around it. Without breaking his pace – no problem for Cider, black dance king of the North London discos – he flicked out a foot and tapped the radio from its precarious site. It turned neatly in the air and dropped into a tray of sludge that had been drained from the engine before disassembly.

Cider suddenly felt a whole lot better.

FIVE

Tina was still at the flat when Nick arrived home that evening. Small and squalid as the place was, it was preferable to the familiar suburbs and the neat house that had suddenly become a museum of memories for her. On his way home, Nick collected a bottle of cheap wine from the all-hours Indian store a couple of blocks away. He didn't much like the stuff and, if the truth were known, neither did Carol; but she had aspirations to social betterment, and considered wine with their evening meal one of the first steps to her goal.

Nick took a beer from the refrigerator. Tina was in much better shape now. She'd decided that she was ready to face the house again, and could stop telling them how good they'd been to her over the last couple of days.

'No,' Tina said. 'Really, I mean it. You've both been great.'

'Great?' said Carol, exaggerating her surprise. 'A bed for two nights? It's hardly what you'd call pain and hardship, is it?'

'It's been an inconvenience for you, I know.' She turned to Nick. 'I'm sorry you've been sleeping on the sofa. But I do appreciate it.'

Not sleeping would be more accurate, Nick thought, but shrugged and said, 'It's been no bother.'

'I need your help, believe me. But I'm not going to start on all that again.'

'That doesn't matter,' Carol said. 'We don't mind. Think of it as being at home, if you like.'

'Thanks. I'll remember that.' She lifted her glass, so far untouched. 'In fact, thanks to both of you.'

There was a little rude noise as Nick opened his beer, and out of the corner of his eye he could see Carol frown as he drank from the can.

'Are you sure you'll be all right?' Nick asked Tina.

'I won't be on my own. My mother's coming over tonight and she'll be staying until the difficult bit's over – whenever that is. I told her to get ready for a long stay.' Tina glanced at her watch and then looked again, in disbelief.

'Is that the time?' she said with mild incredulity. 'I didn't think it was much after four. Honestly, I seem to have lost track.'

'I wasn't hinting,' Nick said.

'No, but really, I'll have to go. My mother will be at the house already.'

'How will she get in?' Carol asked.

'She's got her own key. But I must go, or she'll be worrying.'

Carol looked enquiringly towards Nick, but he was already getting to his feet.

For the first time that he could recall, Nick was selfconscious about the van. But Tina, who was used to better, didn't seem to mind, actually smiling at the clatter as loose objects migrated across the rear as they turned or pulled up the lights. She was almost relaxed, and Nick began to feel a new respect for her. He'd not even seen Greg much more than once every couple of months over the last year – he felt guilty about that now – and his was a loss that came in sharp, poignant waves. But the sudden gap in her life must be faced hour by hour, with no escape even through the night.

'Your mother staying until after the baby's born?' Nick asked, as they turned into the long road that would lead them out to the suburbs. It might have been an insensitive question, but he felt a strange rapport with Tina that he'd never experienced before.

'Probably, or else I'll go and stay with her. But I think I'd prefer to be in my own place. You know what it's like, after you've left home.'

'Yeah,' Nick said with feeling. 'You don't mind me asking?'

'Of course not. Why should I?'

'Bit personal, that's all. Just in case you didn't want to think about it right now.'

'I can't run away from it, so I might as well be pleased at the only good thing that's going to come out of all this. Not that it compensates in any way, though. I was trying to explain that to Carol.'

Nick changed down as they fell in behind a Morris Traveller that was chugging along at little more then twenty-five.

'Explain what?' he said.

'Nothing, really. But when I told her about the baby, she seemed to think that it would make up for everything. Do you see what I mean?'

The road was widening into a dual carriageway. Nick indicated and swung out into the overtaking lane, stamping a little harder on the accelerator than he really needed to. 'I think she's slipping, if she didn't get in a line about insurance, mortgages and pension schemes.'

A lorry's lights filled his rearview mirror, and he pulled back to let it pass. As the juggernaut thundered by, the pause in the conversation gave him a moment to think; he realized in horror that his self-pitying outburst must have sounded like an insensitive jeer at Tina's own predicament.

'Oh, shit!' he said and then, as soon as he could be heard over the diminishing engine roar, 'I didn't mean it that way, Tina, honestly.'

47

'It's all right,' Tina said, cutting across his stammering apology, 'I know what you meant.'

'I wasn't talking about you.'

'I know. I've said, it's all right.'

They drove on in silence for a while. Nick didn't want to speak again because he feared another misunderstanding; also he suspected that her silence showed that her protests of comprehension concealed a real hurt. But in the end it was she that broke the silence.

'You're not going to marry her though, are you?'

She'd understood more than he thought. 'She wants me to,' he said.

'It's not enough, Nick. You both deserve better than that. There, now we've both come out with something we shouldn't.' And the atmosphere began to ease again.

Nick gave the idea some thought, as they covered the last mile into the tidy estate, where Greg had happily chained his brief life and his modest wealth. If it was so obvious to Tina, perhaps it was equally obvious to Carol herself; in fact, it was probably obvious to everybody except Nick, who fled from the idea every time it made itself felt in his mind.

They followed the curve of the driveway and drew up outside the modern detached house. Nick felt yet another irrational twinge of guilt, as he thought of how infrequent his visits had been. Several of the house lights were on but the curtains in most of the rooms were still pulled back. The front door was open and light was spilling across the trimmed lawn. The van's brakes protested as they came to a halt, and a silhouette moved into the open doorway in response to the sound.

Nick wasn't too keen to meet Tina's mother. He hadn't seen her since the wedding, and, although they'd had little contact and the woman had been polite enough, Nick had sensed a vibration of disapproval whenever he moved into

48

her space. Slob, the vibration said, no talent and no direction.

Tina got out of the van. She looked enquiringly at Nick, who was preparing to drive off again.

'What's the matter?' she said. 'Aren't you coming in?'

'You'll have things to talk about.'

'Come on, Nick. At least come in for coffee. There's nothing to be embarrassed about.'

'It's not that, but . . . well, it's late, and you've got a lot of sorting out to do. I'll call you tomorrow, see how everything's going.'

His hesitant determination was obvious, so she didn't try to press him any more. 'You're a funny guy, Nick,' she said affectionately, and Nick didn't know how to answer so he just smiled.

He put the van into gear as Tina walked towards her front door, but as it started to move forward the engine stalled. The van was rolling so he dragged on the handbrake and reached for the ignition key to try again, but by this time Tina had come back.

'Nick, I just thought,' she said. 'Can you please at least take a look at the bikes for me, give me some idea of what they're worth?'

He nodded, and she threw a sizable bunch of keys to him. He was halfway out of the van as he caught them, not wishing to seem determinedly unhelpful, but all the same unsure of the likelihood of his being able to give a reliable valuation. He was just about to explain this, but Tina was already gone, the front door left slightly ajar as an invitation for when he had finished.

At least her mother had gone. Nick sorted through the keys on the bunch, trying to pick out the one that would most probably unlock the garage. The Yale key was obviously for the house, and there were a couple of small keys that probably fitted padlocks or suitcase fastenings so

49

they were ruled out. Two keys remained, large and hefty, and in accordance with some unfathomable law of the universe, the first one that he tried was wrong.

The second one worked, but the door still resisted when he tugged. There was a second lock lower down, a security deadlock, fitted flush with the wood and difficult to see in the dim light, but when this had been turned with the other key, the door swung out easily.

There was a Range Rover in the garage, the poor illumination from the small windows revealed as much. He couldn't see any more than this, all around him being no more than a series of indeterminate shapes and obstacles; so he reached out sideways to where he guessed the lightswitch ought to be. He found it after a few seconds' groping, higher and further over than the place he'd expected it.

No bare lightbulb on a cable slung across the rafters for Greg; a cluster of angled spotlights mounted on adjustable runners in the workshop ceiling flared into life, momentarily dazzling after the soft darkness of the night outside.

There was a high bench running along the side wall nearest to the house, obviously placed at the ideal level to work standing up. A couple of lathes and machines for the hand-turning of metal were bolted to the wood, their cabling neatly stapled to the underside of the bench and meeting at a common junction box. Tools were laid out in neat rows between the pieces of apparatus whilst other items were hung on racks or from custom hooks.

The whole setup reflected Greg's capabilities as a tidy and methodical worker, in many ways the complete opposite of Nick. The concrete floor was swept clean and there were patches of washed-out grey; shapes that betrayed old oil spillages which had not been allowed to settle and soak.

There was a certain aura of reverence in here, as if it were Greg's private temple to the gods of purpose and precision. The objects of mystery that were an integral part of such worship stood in the brilliant focus of the spotlights, canvas-shrouded and demanding of awe.

Nick moved into the bright circle and reached for the nearest cover. It came away easily, falling under its own weight from the metal frame that supported it. The cloth revealed a Norton in the early stages of restoration, the metalwork newly refinished. Some of the mechanical parts had been assembled into the machine, bright and slick with fresh grease. Nick nodded in approval. It was a worthwhile job and it was being well handled . . . or, rather, *had* been well handled before it was cut short. The finished bike would have a real value, but there was no way that he could estimate for Tina, what an incomplete job might fetch on the market.

He bundled up the canvas and dropped it across the frame where the saddle would eventually go, and then reached for the other cover. This was probably a trail bike, he thought as the cloth started to fall away; that would at least bring in some kind of price, or even better a straight road machine that could go through an ad in one of the cycle weeklies, because knowing Greg it would be in perfect condition and would be jumped at by any real enthusiast. . . .

The workshop seemed to brighten as the canvas poured onto the floor. Nick had forgotten to hold on, and the hem ran through his fingers freely. He let it go, mesmerized by the light of Greg's Silver Dream.

At first glance it seemed almost featureless: a glittering silver-grey torpedo that was a space-age version of the traditional racing bike. The fairing and the frame were swept into a single flowing line, which seemed to be designed so that the rider's body would fit in and complete the styling, lending his shape to fill out and streamline the overall form. The seat was small, no more than a flat saddle with a raised back support, and the transparent shield was a narrow curved strip, which would direct the air down onto the rider's shoulders for a minimum of forward resistance and a maximum of grip. But nobody would ever ride the machine; rather the two would join together to become a single racing entity.

Nick circled the Silver Dream, impressed by every angle, every curve. This state of rest seemed to be unnatural for it, a constraint of energies which yearned to be released on the open track. The garage, which had previously seemed a polished and sophisticated setup, suddenly became drab and ordinary when compared to its brilliant centrepiece.

He knelt and touched the fairing. It was like cool silk to his hand and was anchored to the rest of the body by a keyed bolt on either side. The bolts were unlocked; the fairing was surprisingly light, lifting easily and hingeing, seat and everything, upward as he pushed. A glance confirmed that the technology within the machine was as daring and unconventional as its outward appearance. The parts and castings were obviously to Greg's unique specifications, and in some cases Nick could only guess at their functions. The last time Nick had seen anything of the racer's components they had been no more than plans and drawings; undeveloped concepts that were so way-out they seemed unlikely ever to come together into a working system. But here it was, Greg's dream made real, this and a growing child as his unintentional farewell to the world.

Nick gathered up the canvas from the floor, and shook it loose before drawing it back over the Silver Dream. The drabness and frustration of an unhappy world seemed to ease back in around him as the racer disappeared from view. He did the same for the other bike before switching off the spotlights and moving towards the access door to the house, ensuring as he went, that the outer door was re-locked.

SIX

No matter what the weather, a funeral is rarely anything other than dismal. Sam Goldwyn is supposed to have commented, on seeing the crowds that appeared at the funeral of his fellow-producer Louis B. Mayer, that people will always turn out for something they enjoy; Greg Freeman, however, had no enemies to delight in his tragedy.

Nick felt uneasy about the patently theatrical mood of the occasion; the sombreness of dress, and the slowness of limousines far larger than his father could really afford. It wasn't Greg's kind of affair, and it bore no trace of his personality; he was reduced to a weight in an anonymous box, around which the slightest display of levity or fondness would seem a gross betrayal.

There were few mourners, but most of Greg's friends had sent flowers which were heaped in a display by the open grave. Nick's father was there alone – his mother had died some years before – silent and preoccupied. Nick wanted to say something to him, but couldn't think what. Cider and Carol were there as well, as much from their own wish to give Nick support. Tina was with her mother.

After the winding drive through acres of cemetery the limousines emerged onto the main road and, freed of the conspicuous hearse, picked up speed as they headed back towards the suburbs. There was to be sherry and probably some plates of tiny triangular sandwiches with the crusts removed. Nick didn't really want to go, but nor did he want simply to slink away and begin to forget; not yet, anyway; so he put up with the tight and out-of-fashion suit for just a little longer.

Tina's mother had arranged the spread, and it was as depressing as he'd expected. Sherry gave Nick a headache, the sausage rolls were cold and greasy, the ham on the sandwiches was like thin shavings of plastic. When nobody was looking his way Nick slipped out of the front door and into the driveway for some fresh air.

The uniformed chauffeurs were lounging against one of the black cars, hands in pockets and conversing casually. They glanced at Nick without comment, and then resumed their talk. The double door to the garage was slightly open, and a car had been squeezed inside to make the most of the available room. He moved around the vehicle, looking anxiously for the bikes; had they been moved, and if so had they been re-set on their stands with sufficient care? At least, that's how he explained his concern to himself, but he was aware that beneath it lay an innocent hunger to look on the lines of the Silver Dream again.

He lifted a corner of the canvas. The machine was still impressive in the daylight, and he thought of his own bike, the yellow Yamaha of dubious pedigree; visually there was no comparison, and if the performance of the Silver Dream even approached the promise of its appearance . . .

'Hi, Nick,' Tina said from the open doorway. Freeman gave a start and looked around.

'Do you know what you're looking at?' Tina said as she walked into the workshop, and Nick guessed that there was more coming, so he didn't answer.

'All the summers in Spain that we never had. Every spare penny that Greg could scrape together went into that machine, along with three years of his life.'

There was no bitterness in her voice, so Nick said, 'It looks a good bike. I've never seen anything like it before.'

She nodded. 'Please take it away, Nick.'

He looked down at the bike again, and then let the corner of the canvas drop.

55

'Might not be too easy,' he said warily. 'We'll have to try to line up a buyer who can see what the bike's worth, someone who wants to race it. That lets out most of the big outfits with all the money, because they stick with their works machines. Most privateers don't have the backing, either. I suppose we could try some of the bike companies, Honda or somebody, see if we can interest them in it as a prototype . . .'

'You don't want it?' Tina said, puzzled.

'I couldn't afford it.'

'You don't have to.'

'Come on, Tina, you said it yourself. Three years and all that money – you're going to need every penny you can get.'

She looked down at the shrouded form. 'Not from that thing. I never want to see another bike. If you want it, it's yours, and if you don't, you can sell it, but please get it out of here. But Nick, I'm warning you. If you ride it, don't trust it. Don't ever trust a bike like Greg did.'

Tina walked back into the house and Nick watched her go, uncertain as to whether he should follow. Of course, she was emotional and probably not entirely rational in her attitudes at the moment; of course she didn't really mean that he should have the Silver Dream, and if she *did* mean it he couldn't possibly accept. Even if he accepted it, the bike was way out of his class and he couldn't hope to afford to run it or race it; and if he raced it, he'd probably blow the whole thing and cause himself immense embarrassment as he did it.

He moved towards the door, then hesitated, and crossed instead to the workbench. He opened a flat shallow drawer, and then another, and another; they contained plans, sketches – including, Nick noted, the original roughs that Greg had shown him more than three years before – letters, and accounts, all concerned with the Silver Dream. He started to gather a few of them together. They would

56

be useful when he began to seek advice on how to dispose of the bike in the best way. He sifted through for anything that seemed relevant, and the bundle of papers on the work surface grew until the drawers were almost empty.

He went back into the house via the kitchen, and on the way ferreted out a plastic carrier bag for the papers. Much to his relief the gloomy party was starting to break up when he arrived in the sitting-room. Carol gave the bag a puzzled glance as they walked out to the car – even Nick had been forced to agree that his Ford van with its innumerable stickers and its uncertain mechanics was hardly a suitable conveyance for a funeral – but she made no comment.

They shared the car home with a couple of Greg's friends that neither of them had met before. They were pretty much of Greg's age and income, and although nothing was said, Nick could sense Carol's embarrassment as the driver turned to drop them in the inhospitable road where they lived. Not, perhaps, what Greg's friends were used to.

Carol went straight into the bedroom when they were inside, unhooking her ear-rings as she moved out of line with the door and towards the dressing-table. Nick looked around, and thought about switching on the radio. Somehow it didn't seem right. He wasn't hungry either, and the too-sweet sherry that he'd sipped out of politeness had taken away any taste for a beer. He was too restless to sit, and there was nowhere he wanted to go.

Sounds of Carol moving around were still coming from the bedroom, and Nick realized that he was still holding his carrier bag full of papers. He looked inside, and pulled at the corner of the nearest sheet. It was an invoice for the materials for some castings, a yellow flimsy dated just over two years before and stamped in red, *paid in full*. Another invoice in the same stationery had a more recent date and no stamp; Nick remembered that the two had come from different drawers, and realized that Greg had probably

57

organized all of his accounts with a care that Nick had rendered pointless when he'd simply scooped the material in handfuls from the bench.

He tipped the papers out onto the floor, and began to separate them into piles. One was for bills that were obviously paid, another for the few bills that seemed to be outstanding; if he found a technical drawing that seemed to be directly related to one of the bills, he laid it by the side of the relevant heap. Letters went into another pile to be glanced over later, as did any drawings that didn't fit in with the layout.

He was covering quite an area when Carol emerged from the bedroom. 'What's this?' she said, automatically slipping into antagonism at the sight of mess and disorder.

'The stuff to do with Greg's bike,' Nick explained, 'the Silver Dream. Tina asked me to have a look at it.'

'Oh,' Carol said, slightly mollified. 'But I thought you'd told her she should get a dealer to value it.'

'She doesn't want to.'

'Then how . . .' Carol began, and then realization dawned. 'Oh, no! Come on, Nick. You're not getting ideas about taking it over.'

' 'Course not,' he said, not very convincingly.

'That's it, isn't it? Tina doesn't want to know, and you're too stupid to know when to keep your hands off. Anybody would think you're hell-bent on going the same way as Greg.'

'I'm looking at the papers for her, that's all.'

Carol was more tired than angry: she hadn't the energy to argue after the rituals of grief.

'And I suppose you expect me to believe that's as far as it goes, do you? Forget it, Nick. I've had enough.' She made a gesture which indicated the small flat – it wasn't much of a gesture, because there wasn't much to cover.

'Look at this place. I mean just look at it. It's tiny, it's

58

scruffy, it's lousy and it isn't even really ours. And this is the place I have to spend half of my life, sitting on my own while you go out and play with bikes! When is it going to stop, Nick? When am I ever going to be able to look forward to anything better? I spend all day on my feet in that lousy store, so we can live in this dump while you play roulette with your life. And just when I think it's coming to an end, you start over!'

'Nobody says I'm starting anything,' Nick said, but Carol could read him better than that.

'Nick,' she pleaded, 'will you listen to me? When you go out of that door I never know if I'll ever see you again. Don't you understand that Greg's dead? Are you just going to go on without even considering that?'

Nick got to his feet and walked through into the kitchen. Carol stared after him. He was immune to persuasion, indifferent to reason.

'You're like a child,' she called, wonderingly, realizing the truth of her own discovery. 'You know that? Nothing more than a child.'

She followed him into the kitchen, unwilling to drop the subject now that she had a hold on it. 'This is as far as I can go, Nick. Because if this is how you're going to carry on, I can see I'll either live in a dump like this forever or else I'll end up like Tina.' Her anger was falling in on itself, becoming misery. 'What about kids and . . . and settling down, finding somewhere that's decent to live?'

'Give it a rest, Carol,' Nick said.

She looked at him for a moment, stopped in her tracks. It seemed that she could entice or persuade without any detectable effect beyond a momentary discomfort. Nick had some inner core of self-obsession, to which she was obviously a second rate consideration.

'Listen,' he said as she began to turn away. 'It's not as

bad as all that. The bike's finished.' But she shook her head, finding the fact less than comforting.

Neither of them raised the subject of the Silver Dream during the rest of the evening – in fact, they conversed very little on any subject at all. The topic only reappeared late that night, when a combination of proximity and a tense, wakeful silence made it unavoidable. For the first time, Nick attempted to put into words the urge that drove him, but he failed. He was insufficiently articulate, and it was impossible to explain to somebody who had never ridden how irresistible was the call to be out there flying, for a brief time at one with the angels. He couldn't lower his sights and allow himself to be tethered to a little patch of land, bound by overpowering obligations and responsibilities that would usher him down the quiet and narrow path to old age and the grave.

Greg had intended to introduce the Silver Dream at Silverstone – a gift to the sub-editors who drafted the headlines in the cycle magazines, and probably the most effective way imaginable to launch a new design. The Grand Prix attracted the top riders from every nation, and the consequent press coverage was phenomenal, making the competition quite unlike any other in the calendar. It seemed that Greg had intended to ask for Nick's advice in selecting a rider; the idea flattered him, but at the same time he was depressed as he faced the fact that Silverstone was out of his class.

McBride would undoubtedly be riding at Silverstone. Bruce McBride, whom God had touched and blessed to be a winner, whilst Nick Freeman . . . Still, for a while the Silver Dream was in his hands, and as long as the future remained comfortingly remote, any dream was possible.

'Greg didn't actually ask *you* to ride it, did he?' Carol said as they lay looking up at the faint shadows of the streetlights on the bedroom ceiling, reassured by Nick's insistence that he understood her feelings.

'No,' Nick admitted. 'I never made it far enough. I'd stand about as much chance as Roy Rogers on Trigger. And he's been stuffed for ten years.' And then they both started to laugh, quietly but with a great shaking of the mattress.

'So the bike's too good for you,' Carol said, grabbing at the weakness and trying to exploit it for what it was worth. 'What are you going to do with it?'

'Probably wouldn't even qualify.'

'What are you going to *do*?' Carol insisted, an edge of worry creeping into her voice.

'Don't know yet.'

'Well, I do. You can sell the bloody thing.'

'I haven't even tested it.' She was starting to get out of the bed, and Nick caught her arm. 'Carol, wait a minute.'

'Either you get rid of it, or I go. I mean it, Nick.'

He didn't answer, instead he reached out to hold her. She returned without resistance, and her composure began to dissolve. But she'd made her ultimatum, and now, it seemed, as the sadness welled up inside her, she knew the choice that he would make.

SEVEN

Cider noted that Nick was not late into the garage the next morning; if anything he was early, because his van was already parked in its usual inconvenient and conspicuous place when Cider arrived. Funeral notwithstanding, Nick's timekeeping record was one of the worst in the plant, and he needed all of the plus-points that he could gather. 'You realize it's not me,' Wiggins would explain, 'but the front office has been getting on my back again and they say it's got to stop . . .'

But Nick wasn't in the stores when Cider looked around for him. The girl who was on the customer sales counter gave him her usual blank look, and Cider decided that it wasn't worth the effort of enquiry. Her father worked in the coachbuilding shop, and was a fervent member of the National Front with a head you could drive nails into without fear of serious damage. Her rare exchanges with Cider never rose above unhelpful monosyllables.

He went to his bay and consulted his work sheet for the first job of the day, a yellow Mercedes with electrics trouble. He collected the keys from the office and brought the car into the bay; most of the other mechanics were in and working by now, and as Cider unlocked the hood on the Mercedes and got out, he could hear the abrupt start of the high-treble noise of Jack Davis' ever-present radio.

Freeman appeared some time later, his stores coat slung casually over his shoulder. 'Don't tell me,' Cider said, 'you've come as Frank Sinatra.'

'If only he had half my style. Guess what I've been doing.'

'If I was interested in that kind of thing, I'd buy a special magazine for it. The kind they don't sell to anybody under eighteen.'

'Come on, Cider. Have a guess.'

He gave a weary sigh. 'You've found out that if you pee on a live socket a light shines out your ass.'

'Better than that. I brought the bike in.'

'Headline news. Nick Freeman's famous Yamaha still hanging together. Thousands gather to witness miracle.'

'Not the Yamaha. The Silver Dream.'

'Greg's bike?' Cider said, and Nick nodded. 'So what?'

This obviously wasn't the reaction that Nick had hoped for. 'So what? Is that all you're going to say, so what?'

'I already said it. I'm done with getting wrapped up in your weird fantasies.' Cider plunged under the hood of the Mercedes with excessive zeal, his determination fighting down his interest.

'At least ask me about the B.H.P.'

'I don't want to know about the B.H.P.,' Cider's voice came muffled by the hood.

'Cider, what's the matter with you?'

Cider emerged, shaking his head regretfully. 'Okay. What's the horsepower?'

Nick pulled a folded piece of paper out of his pocket, a summary of the Silver Dream's specifications. 'Hundred and forty,' he read off.

Cider shrugged. It was good, but by no means unheard of. 'So it's got disc valves. Wow.'

'You haven't heard the frame weight. It'll kill you.'

'All right, tell me and commit the perfect crime. They'll never find the murder weapon.'

'Fourteen pounds.'

'Fourteen assholes,' Cider snorted. Normal bike frame-weight was more like twenty-five. There was a limit to the amount that you could shave off before the structure was

63

so weakened as to be useless. 'Don't tell me, it's made out of toilet rolls.'

Nick held out the specification sheet as if in challenge, and Cider took it. 'It's space technology, carbon fibre and stuff like that. Greg redesigned the frame from scratch to suit the materials. There's no sub-frame at all, and he got somebody to do a computer run for him to calculate how to get all the stresses redistributed.'

Cider stared at the paper, the Mercedes momentarily forgotten. If the technology of the rest of the bike matched the frame, the one-forty B.H.P. would be pulling almost half the load. Nick had walked off in the direction of the storeroom and Cider, like a fish on a line, began to follow.

He did a neat sidestep to avoid bumping into Wiggins, as the garage foreman came into the workshop.

'Hey,' Wiggins said. 'Where the hell do you think you're going?'

'Don't know for sure, man,' Cider said without stopping, his eyes still on the paper. 'Looks like it could be a long way . . .'

Jack Davis saw Cider coming, and quickly rescued his radio. Wiggins came level and said, 'Where's he going, Jack?'

'Where does he always go?' Davis said, sensing an opportunity to make trouble for somebody. 'The hobby corner. I think it used to be the stores.'

'Productivity in this place is a joke,' Wiggins said, bitter more than anything else at his own lack of authority.

'No joke when it affects the bonus, Mister Wiggins.'

Wiggins hesitated, Davis was looking at him evenly, and he thought about how badly a non-assertive foreman might appear to the front office.

'Well,' Davis said. 'Am I right?'

'Yes,' said Wiggins, his resolve growing. 'Yes, you're

64

right.' And he set off after Cider with an unusually grim expression.

'You're trying to tell me this machine's actually *finished*?' Cider demanded in disbelief, as he and Nick walked down one of the alleys of Dexion shelving in the vast stores area.

'I'm not trying to tell you anything. You said you weren't interested.' Nick gave Cider a complacent smile, and picked the specifications sheet out of the air as Cider waved it.

'Stop screwing about, Nick. You can't dump this in somebody's lap and then go wandering off without as much as an explanation.'

'I'm *sorry*, Cider,' Nick said with affected concern. 'If I'd known I was going to spoil your day, I wouldn't have bothered.'

'Look, smart-ass Freeman, is the bike finished or is this piece of paper just somebody's dream for a machine that will work like water runs uphill?'

'It's finished. It's working.'

'Holy shit,' Cider said with due reverence. 'Where did Greg get that kind of money?'

'The mag-castings were done at the company he worked for, and he got a friend to do the mouldings. You know the kind of thing, trading favours. When he *had* to pay for something – like there's some fancy electrical stuff in there – he paid for it, but most of the bike was put together with free help. That's why none of the big bike companies know anything about it.'

'You said it's working. Has it run yet?'

'Once, last week. I found some notes, but I'm not sure what most of them mean.' They turned at the end of the alley near to the door of the stockroom which was the yellow Yamaha's unofficial garage space. 'Now,' Nick said, 'are you ready for this? He was going to enter it at Silverstone.'

'*Silverstone?*' Cider said, with the blank dismay of a home movie freak who had just been handed a Panavision camera. He was about to say something else, when he turned at the sound of his name.

Wiggins was hurrying down the metal alley after them, his clipboard in his hand and a flush of exertion on his pale unhealthy skin.

'Look,' he said breathlessly as he caught up with them, 'you two will have to get something straight.'

Cider was less than humble; he responded as if Wiggins were bringing a tiresome interruption to important work. 'Shit, Wiggy,' he said, using the nickname that Wiggins detested, 'what is it now?'

'Don't you shit-Wiggy me,' Wiggins warned.

'Don't you shit-Wiggy *anybody*,' Nick told Cider in an obvious copy of Wiggins' indignation. 'It's very rude.'

'Jack Davis,' Wiggins said firmly, determined to exert some kind of authority in the face of anarchy, 'has got a serious complaint.'

'I know,' said Cider. 'But I thought he was going to get it lanced.'

'Someone said it was turning green,' Nick added helpfully.

'Will you knock it off!'

'Not me, man,' Cider said. 'I wouldn't touch it.'

'Me neither,' said Nick. 'It's one of the nastiest complaints I've ever seen.'

'Leave it long enough, and it'll drop off. Might as well just let it hang if it's doing nobody any harm.'

'Right,' Wiggins said sharply. The indignation that he had forced himself to feel on behalf of his employer had now boiled over into real anger. 'If you're not back in two minutes, Cider, I'm taking Davis's complaint to the management.' With that he turned and stalked off.

Cider watched him go. 'Maybe *they*'*ll* knock it off for him,' he said.

Nick fished the stockroom key out of his pocket. 'You ready for this?' he said.

'What is this, talent night? Open the door.'

Nick pushed the door open and stepped aside to let Cider pass. Inside the stockroom the Silver Dream was standing uncovered, dazzling and incongruous in such mundane surroundings.

Cider hesitated, transfixed, and then took a cautious step across the threshold. Nick noted with satisfaction that the sequence of rapture he'd experienced was repeating itself as Cider walked around the machine and then reached out to touch it lightly, as if some rough contact might cause it to lose substance and dissolve back into the alien dimension from which it had come.

'It's not a bike,' he said, pleased and impressed. 'It's a work of art. It's something else.' He looked up at Nick sharply. 'Wait a minute. I hope I don't get the idea that you want to race this thing.'

'No, of course not,' said Nick. 'Although . . .'

'Although what?'

'I was thinking of trying a few practice laps. You know, see how it goes.'

'See how it goes? *You?* With the performance that thing's got? What makes you think you can learn to fly kites and then go and pilot Concorde?'

'It's not as bad as that.'

'But it *is*. A top international rider would think twice.'

'You'll have to learn it too, of course,' Nick went on as if he hadn't heard. 'But it shouldn't—'

'*Learn* it?' Cider said in amazement. '*Learn* it? Your brother had an engineering degree, and most of what I know I learned on ten-year-old wrecks! That bike's got too much class. It needs a backup team the size of Suzuki.'

67

'And all it's got is you.'

Shaking his head slowly, Cider said, 'You're crazy, you know that?'

'Brands Hatch is open tomorrow. What do you say?'

'No way.'

'Pick you up at six?'

'No, I said. What's the matter, you can't understand a simple statement?'

EIGHT

It was a grey and misty Saturday morning, barely light as they set out to beat the city traffic and get clear of the centre early. Driving south-east, the urban sprawl began to give way to the open rolling greens of the North Downs and at this time the roads were still quiet, shared only with a few long-haul lorries and a light trickle of loaded holiday traffic for the south coast and the ferries.

Cider feigned deep discontent, but he knew when he was hooked. The magic of the Silver Dream had ensnared him as surely as it had ensnared Nick, and so he endured – admittedly with bad graces – the damp, penetrating chill of the morning and the oppressive vastness of the empty track, as they rolled the Silver Dream from the back of the van and funnelled a couple of pints of fuel into the tank for an engine test.

Nick had climbed into his pads and leathers in the now-empty van, and came out to help with the starting of the Silver Dream. The engine fired at the first turn, despite the fact that this was only the second time that it had been tried off the workbench, and as Nick swung his leg across the all-enveloping fairing and got comfortable on the tiny saddle Cider said, 'Take it easy, and for Christ's sake watch the counter. It's that readout, there.'

'I know where the rev counter is.'

'I sometimes wonder. Take it nice and slow the first time round, and if anything doesn't feel right you come straight in.'

Nick twisted the throttle a couple of times. The bike didn't roar in a noisy explosion of energy, but simply purred more loudly and with greater confidence. He moved

69

into gear, and let it roll. For a few seconds he kept his legs out at the sides, boots trailing only a couple of inches above the ground as he got the feel and balance of the bike and then, finding no wobble or unevenness, he brought his legs in and began to increase the power.

Cider fished out his stopwatch as Nick approached the bend, for once moving sedately and with caution. There was no point in timing the laps yet, not when they weren't trying for speed, and besides he'd done his usual trick of leaving the watch running the last time he'd used it so that the spring had wound down. It happened every time Nick came limping across the line with a shattered machine.

It seemed a while before the Silver Dream made its reappearance. Cider walked over to the trackside barrier, a wall of low blocks painted with advertisers' messages and dampened by the morning dew, and sat on it. He looked up the track to the curve beyond the empty pits and saw Nick coming around into the straight, barely leaning at all as he took the corner smoothly.

Somebody was in the grandstand opposite, obvious amidst the emptiness. The figure was descending from the upper bleachers watching as the Silver Dream cruised past, engine note beginning to rise as Freeman gained confidence in his handling of the machine. He didn't slow as he approached so Cider looked across the track for some feature on which he could fix his eyes for a reliable and constant reading on the watch as the bike cut across his vision on each lap.

The Silver Dream was really moving as, for a fraction of a second, it cut between Cider and his chosen letter in the message on the opposite barrier. He clicked the watch automatically; his reaction time would cancel out when he stopped it again.

Nick leaned much harder into the bend, his knee thrusting out at an angle and sweeping close to the ground as the centrifugal forces were cancelled out. The figure was still in the grandstand, and seemed to be looking down the track after the Silver Dream.

It was the American girl who tagged along with the McBride outfit, dressed in a one-piece leather which would make her look part of the team in spite of the fact that she probably didn't know one end of a bike from the other. Cider smiled as he recognized her. The girl saw him and smiled back. Did this mean that McBride would be turning up at the track today as well? Probably so, and Cider gave a little inward groan. All he needed was for Nick to start getting showy in front of the girl and burn up the engine, or else pour in too much power and lose it on one of the bends.

Behind Cider the first vehicles of the Trans-World travelling circus were pulling into the pits. He didn't need binoculars to be able to see that McBride and his team-mates were leading the procession in what seemed like an immense American saloon, but which by transatlantic standards was probably no more than a modest tourer.

Nick shrieked past at high speed, and Cider swore. He'd missed operating the stopwatch, momentarily distracted as the girl ran down the steps from the grandstand towards the backup trucks. Now he'd have to reset the watch on the next pass; it seemed, even without timing, that Nick was making good speed. Don't blow it, you bastard, Cider thought.

The next time Nick came around, Cider was ready. He set the watch and waited, hearing the dying roar as the Silver Dream disappeared from his eyeline, listening for the occasional echo to be carried from the further parts of the track, watching for the bike's reappearance beyond the grandstand.

Down it came, and Cider fixed his gaze and reacted as the blur passed before him. He looked at the time, doing a quick calculation, and when he looked up with a frown Nick was already out of sight again.

They had poured only a small amount of fuel into the tank, and Nick would soon have to slow down and come in or else face another ignominious marooning with a dead bike. On the next approach he cut the throttle and cruised the last couple of hundred yards before braking.

Nick swung the bike around in a neat half-circle to bring it to Cider, seemingly reluctant to stop completely. He pushed up his visor and grinned.

'How was it?' he said.

Cider indicated the rev counter. 'Were you red-lining that needle?' he said suspiciously.

'Me?' said Nick with exaggerated innocence. 'Would I do a thing like that?'

'You want it in a word?'

'Well, I didn't. I was miles off. What's on the clock?'

Cider held out the stopwatch for Nick to look as he dismounted. On the pits sliproad Cider could see McBride's car, and it was heading towards them. 'This is the reading from that last lap.'

'So what?' Nick said, trying to be casual about it and only just succeeding. 'The lap record here's two seconds faster than that.'

'And your best is three seconds slower.'

Nick couldn't be flip about it any longer. 'You know,' he said, 'you're right.'

A seemingly endless length of motor body slid alongside them. The car's windows were open, and the radio was making more noise than the engine. McBride was driving and Nichols and Mendoza, his two Trans-World team riders, were lounging next to him.

'Good morning, early birds!' McBride said brightly. If he remembered the mild clash of their last meeting, he

72

showed no sign of it; not so Nick, whose face hardened as he saw the American.

'Saw you on the track,' McBride went on. 'What the hell *is* that thing?'

Cider gave Nick a warning glance, wondering if he would react to McBride's presence, or his interest in the machine, or his casual way of referring to it.

'It's a prototype,' Nick said quietly.

'Mind if I take a look?' McBride said, opening the car door and sliding out. As if on cue from their leader, Mendoza and Nichols spilled after him. Nick could hardly refuse without seeming childish, but he felt none of the cameraderie towards any of the Trans-World team that normally exists between riders. Reluctantly, he assented.

'Hey, look who it is!' Mendoza shouted, and all heads turned to the girl who was walking across the track towards them. She grinned and waved.

'Julie!' McBride shouted, and ran around the car towards her. Nick was left supporting the Silver Dream, an annoyed and unwilling spectator to the horseplay. McBride was obviously used to having people wait around for him, and he wasn't about to break the habit for somebody as unimportant as Nick Freeman.

McBride had lifted Julie off her feet and was swinging her around, and she was laughing and calling for help. McBride began to call for help as well and so Mendoza ran over and took Julie from him, to keep the laughter and the protests going.

Trans-World's top rider, rated number four in the field and on the way up. And he knew it. He strolled back to the Silver Dream, and glanced at Cider. 'Do you mind?' he said.

'Sure,' Cider said cautiously. 'Why not?'

McBride climbed into the saddle and gripped the

handlebars to get the feel of the machine. Nichols, Mendoza and Julie came around as well.

'If I didn't know better,' McBride said, surprised, 'I'd say that somebody took the frame out. I don't think I've ever felt a bike as light as this.' He looked at Nick with a new interest. 'Forgive me for asking, but where in hell—'

'—did a schmuck like me get a dream like this?'

Oh, Christ, thought Cider.

'I didn't say that,' McBride protested.

'No, I said it.'

The jocularity had gone from the two backup riders, their faces hard. Julie seemed anxious, embarrassed by the sudden injection of bad feeling. Only McBride seemed to be relaxed and unruffled.

'Come on, Nick,' Cider said. 'He wasn't trying to get to you.'

'Excuse me,' McBride said, leaning forward and dusting something off Nick's shoulder. 'That wouldn't be a chip I see, would it, Freeman?' This time he didn't need to look for the name on the leathers.

'Can I have my bike back?' Nick said evenly.

McBride looked down at the Silver Dream, and smiled a quiet smile to himself. The train of thought was obvious; Freeman's a child with a child's obsessive nature, and it would be unkind and unworthy of McBride to put him down or argue with him. 'Sure,' he said, and dismounted, giving the weight of the bike to Cider.

'You racing this afternoon?' Cider said to break the silence.

'Just in the trophy,' McBride said amiably, and turned to Nick. 'See you on the track.'

'Not if I see you first.'

This was pushing it. Nick resented the indulgent patronage, and McBride was quickly using up his supply of tolerance. Cider cut in again with, 'We're here to test the bike, that's all,' and McBride turned abruptly to Julie.

'Would you like some breakfast?' he said.

She hesitated for a moment. 'Go on ahead. I'll catch you up.'

McBride nodded, and moved towards his car, closely followed by Nichols and Mendoza. None of them was smiling.

Cider found that he had been left close to Julie. Nick was a few yards away, leaning on the wall and watching as the car began its turn.

'Bet you never saw anything like this before,' Cider said, aware of how lame it must sound. Julie smiled, but it was a politeness which didn't touch the eyes. She was looking towards Nick.

'I've seen a lot of motorcycles,' she said. 'Excuse me.'

Nick didn't deliberately ignore her, but he was still preoccupied with his own thoughts and the sight of the distant vehicle as it drew in with the Trans-World entourage. She waited until he looked around.

'Can I ask you something?' she said, and then went on without waiting for an answer. 'Maybe you've got reasons, or maybe you've got some strange ideas of your own, but I'd sure like to know what's eating you. Bruce McBride's a decent guy and a good rider, and whatever it is you've got against him he's done nothing to deserve it.'

'Have you known him long?'

'What does that have to do with anything?'

'Ask him how Carl Schultz is these days. Then ask him who Jimmy Prince used to be.'

Even Nick was surprised at her reaction. She stiffened as if slapped, and the colour seemed to drain from her tan for a couple of seconds before boiling back, red and angry.

'I know who Jimmy Prince used to be,' she said tightly,

75

'but I doubt if you do. If I were you, I'd confine my comments to things I understand.'

She turned away and began the long walk back to the Trans-World enclave. Other vehicles were appearing on the course in preparation for the meeting later that day; a couple of bikes were being rolled out for testing.

'Why don't you shove it?' Nick said, loudly enough for her to hear.

She walked on, ignoring the remark.

Cider said, 'You're looking for a punch in the mouth, right?'

'From McBride? People like that make me want to throw up.'

'Oh, that explains everything. For a minute, I thought you were being unreasonable.'

'Come on, Cider,' Nick said angrily. 'You know it and I know it, that is the most selfish bastard on two wheels. There are at least two riders who are vegetables because of the way he cut them up on the track. What about Langley at that last meeting? McBride isn't interested in what kind of mess he leaves behind – all he cares about is coming first.'

'Yeah,' Cider said drily. 'I know the type.'

NINE

The British Isles has never quite managed to grasp the concept of the motel. But then, a country so dedicated to inconvenience and discomfort could hardly be expected to wholeheartedly embrace such a notion. When Cider and Nick decided to stay to watch the afternoon meeting and Cider suggested that they should go over to the motel for a sandwich and a drink, both knew what they were in for; a fight through an overcrowded bar with inadequate service, not enough seats and too much muzak, gassy beer and limp white bread stuffed with all the bleaches and poisons that modern technology could legally include.

They wheeled the Silver Dream into the back of the van and clamped it down, then fixed the back doors in place with a new padlock bought for the purpose. When they arrived at the motel and found a space in the tightly-packed car park, Cider took the added precaution of removing the rotor arm from the van's engine. Even so, the Silver Dream seemed disturbingly unprotected, a depressing sign of the inadequate backup which was all that they could manage.

'We must be crazy,' Cider said.

'*That's* the word I was trying to think of,' said Nick.

The chic élite of the racing set were to be found in the bar amidst a great babbling crowd of journalists and hangers-on. McBride was somewhere in the middle of a spreading wheel of attention from his entourage, swapping jokes with his team-mates which caused far greater waves of hilarity than the humour or the skill in telling could justify. Cider and Nick squeezed and eased their way towards the bar, where a man and a girl were demonstrating their skill at looking the other way from everybody at once.

A small handwritten sign told them that sandwiches were available from a counter in the cocktail lounge, and Cider said he'd get the food if Nick would see to the drinks. Nick readily agreed; it seemed that Cider could glide through dense crowds like a shadow, something that he always attributed to practice on over populated disco floors.

Nick watched him go, impressed by his grace, and then turned back to the bar. Both of the staff were at the far end, picking glasses out of the air and refilling them automatically and with no acknowledgement of fairness or order. This could take a while.

Through the bar chatter came McBride's voice, now answering journalists' questions but still keeping the light, jokey tone of a few moments before.

'Can you tell us what you think of the idea of compulsory training for people using bikes on the road?' somebody called out.

'Can *you* tell us your name and your newspaper, please?' Al Peterson, McBride's manager and the steering intelligence of Trans-World, threw back at the reporter. Even in this casual gathering the cold-eyed and angular Peterson was keeping control, and giving McBride a moment to come up with a non-controversial answer.

'Uh . . . Simon Addison. *The Banner.*'

'I'm not really in favour of anything that's compulsory,' McBride said and there was an amused murmur, not because he'd made a joke but because one had been expected. 'I never had any training, but then I never ride a bike on the roads, either.'

'Watch him this afternoon,' Nichols advised, 'and you'll find out why.' Peterson gave him a sharp look.

'No, it's a serious problem. I really think the present limit for unqualified riders – what is it now, two-fifty? I think that's too high. A kid with a bike, that can do anything up to a hundred, isn't going to feel that there's any pressure on him to get trained and tested on his roadcraft, if all he has to do is go on showing his learner plates. Now, I don't know what you'll think of my opinion as a non-resident' – laughter – 'but I like to think I'm kind of qualified on something like this, and I think the plans to drop your learner-limit to one-fifty are pretty sound.'

The reporter, a hesitant youth in a creased leather jacket, nodded and smiled his thanks.

'Tom Patterson, *Race Bike Monthly*. You missed out on the meetings in Holland last week so you didn't get involved in the riders' strike there. What do you think of the bans and the fines that are being talked about?'

'Well, firstly, I don't think you can punish a rider for choosing not to ride if he thinks conditions are too dangerous. Having said that, I've ridden the Dutch courses a few times and I've found them as safe as any. But I wasn't there and I don't know what the conditions were like, so it isn't really fair to ask me.'

So it went on, some questions more pointed than others. McBride's answers were solid and sensible, touched with an impersonal dullness that suggested that the opinions and assertions were mostly the results of a preparatory briefing from Peterson; for once the asshole was controlling himself and doing a PR job for his sponsors.

Still no response from behind the bar, but at least the barman was working along in the right direction. There was a girl with an empty glass a little further down the rail from Nick – but wait a minute, it wasn't just *a* girl, it was McBride's girl, her back towards him. If she turned now, Nick could be in for an unbearable few minutes of stony disapproval until one or other of them was served. He moved as close as he could manage against the press of the crowd and said, 'My friend says I owe you an apology.'

She turned in surprise, and he could almost see the

wheels in her mind clicking over as he registered. 'Your friend is right,' she said.

'Can I buy you a drink?'

'Shove it. I think that's the expression the smart set use around here.'

'I said I'm sorry,' he told her quickly as she began to turn away again.

Her eyebrows raised. 'You did? Must be that I'm going deaf, or something. All I heard was that your *friend* thinks you should apologize.'

'I'm sorry,' Nick said with all the sincerity he could muster, which on reflection didn't seem to be very much. It certainly wasn't enough to impress her.

'Thank you,' she said with icy grace. 'And now this conversation, if you can dignify it with the name, is at an end.'

He couldn't let it go as easily as that. She was facing away from him, but she still couldn't help hearing. 'On the track this morning . . . you said something.'

'It's a habit of mine. I open my mouth and entire sentences come out. You should try it.'

'You said you knew Jimmy Prince.' If she reacted at all, she covered it with an irritated wave of her glass to catch the barman's attention. It didn't work. 'I used to follow him around. He was a sort of . . . well, I suppose you'd say he was an idol of mine. Whenever I could get the time off to get to where he was riding, I'd go. I got into the whole race thing because I could see what he was, and I wanted to be like him. I was in the crowd on the day he died.'

'That's a distinction you share with thousands of others.'

'Yes, well, Bruce McBride was riding too, and—'

'Excuse me,' she said, and tried to push her way out from the bar. The mass of people trying to do exactly the opposite was impenetrable, and when Nick looked up he

80

realized, with a surge of disbelief, that the barman was looking straight at him with an expression of polite enquiry.

'No, wait,' Nick said quickly, and pushed Julie's glass across to keep the barman occupied. He inspected the drops in the bottom and moved off to refill it with more of the same. 'I'm an old-fashioned chauvinist, so I'll pay,' he went on, and seeing that this was a less than persuasive added, 'but I'm trying to kick the habit you can get me a large scotch if you like.'

The barman was returning Julie's glass and heard the order. He picked a glass from somewhere under the bar and moved over to the whisky optic, as Nick braced himself for the inescapable blast.

She almost smiled. She was far from pleased, but the heat had gone from her anger, and then, suddenly, the crowd seemed to ripple and Cider was back with them carrying sandwiches wrapped in serviettes.

'I got the food, so where's my booze?' he said.

Nick turned to the barman. 'A Bloody Mary for the racist, here.'

Cider gave a half-bow in Julie's direction – or, at least, as much as he could manage under the circumstances. 'Hello again,' he said. 'You're the second most beautiful thing I've seen today.'

'I suppose I ought to be offended,' she said, warming to his easy charm, 'but if you're talking about that bike of yours I'll have to take it with good grace. That machine's really something else, right?'

'Lady, I'm getting to like you more and more. My name's Cider but I never drink the stuff.'

'My name's Julie Prince and I'm buying you a Bloody Mary.'

As she paid the barman, Cider watched Nick's reaction to the name. It was, considering, quite restrained; just a swallow and a bulging of the eyes, no actual steam coming out of the ears.

They chatted for a while, the usual inane pleasantries of people who don't know each other very well and who don't expect to. They talked about London, and the appalling costs of accommodation – hardly mentioning racing at all. After ten minutes or so there was a stirring as the Trans-World group rose around McBride and began to move with him towards the door. Others started to look at their watches and finish their drinks in a hurry, and Nick said, 'I suppose you'll have to be going.'

Julie shrugged. 'I've got my own transport to get me back to the track,' she said, 'and sometimes it can be really dull fighting your way through the crowds you get around Bruce. It can take him a quarter of an hour to cover a hundred yards when the autograph hunters all gang up.'

'Must be pretty annoying.'

'Not really. He loves every minute of it.'

'I meant for you.'

She looked at Nick, seeming to be both pleased and surprised that, for once, somebody was not ignoring her and talking only of McBride. 'I can handle it,' she said.

Julie declined another drink and they moved towards the motel car-park a few minutes later. The crowd in the bar was noticeably thinner and there were plenty of spaces for vehicles outside as people drifted back towards the track for the race preparations, or to get an advantageous view of the course. Julie's car was an open-topped MG, and Nick walked over to it with her as Cider lifted the hood on the van to replace the rotor arm.

'Nice,' Nick said as she unzipped the cover. 'Must have cost you quite a bit.'

'The car was nothing compared to the insurance. I almost had to sell one to pay for the other.'

'I know what you mean. See you in the stands?'

She gave him a sideways glance, her expression amused and thoughtful. 'Maybe,' she said, and turned the ignition. The engine caught at the first attempt and Nick stepped aside as she reversed out of her space and gunned across the car park.

The dull mists of the morning had given way to a mild and fairly agreeable afternoon. The stands began to fill early, but they had no trouble getting reasonable seats; a few minutes before the first race Julie appeared. They made room so that she could sit between them; it seemed that she'd had enough of being on the periphery of the activity in the pits and wanted to see some of the action from above ground-level for once.

Nick saw from his programme that Stoddard would be riding in the Trophy race. 'It'll give me somebody to root for,' he told Julie without expression, and fortunately she didn't rise to the obvious bait.

Cider went off for some ice creams, complaining that he was looked on as nothing more then a human chuck wagon, and when he got back Julie and Nick were chatting. The chequered flag was going down as he leaned across the row to hand out the ices, and when he momentarily blocked Julie's view Nick said, 'Have some respect, Cider. Don't you know you're sitting next to a doctor?'

'Really?' Cider said, looking around. 'Where?'

'Not really a doctor,' Julie explained. 'Just a medical student.'

'Great stuff. Have to have you around to look at Jack Davis's complaint. Word is that it'll make medical history.'

She was obviously puzzled, so Nick said, 'Ignore him. He won't go away, but it's still worth a try.'

'That's where you're wrong,' Cider said, settling back in his seat and looking down the track towards where several riders were being bump-started in preparation for the main event of the afternoon. 'I'll be leaving right after this race.'

'How am I going to get home?' Nick protested, and Cider absorbed his meaning without any change of expression. Obviously he was enjoying the girl's company and didn't want to leave, and whilst it wasn't up to Cider to make judgements on the fairness or the morality of his friend's behaviour, he wasn't about to put major obstacles in his way, either.

'Nothing wrong with the train,' he said. 'My turn with the van, remember?'

'Yeah,' Nick said, 'thanks.' And they turned their attention to the track as the riders lined up for the start of the Trophy race.

McBride began badly, as he often seemed to do; his speciality was not in fast starts, but in an opportunistic hopping up through the field as the chances came. Nick had his own ideas about the methods that Trans-World used to ensure that their star rider came out in front; he'd seen them in action a couple of times, and whilst there was nothing substantial enough to support an accusation before the marshals or any of the controlling boards, he was certain in his own mind that McBride alone would have considerably less success than McBride in a team.

Not that he wasn't a good rider, even, Nick grudgingly had to admit, a brilliant one; but with two team-mates whose unofficial job was as much to obstruct the opposition as to gain credit for themselves, it was difficult to see how McBride could lose.

There was some evidence of it on the third lap, Nichols and Mendoza taking a bend side-by-side with Stoddard behind them, unable to swing out far enough to pass them and still maintain his speed. McBride was ahead and closing in on the three leaders, Dennison out in front with Evans and Le Fours jockeying for second place. McBride would have to beat them on his own, but at least the field had been swept clear of any distraction.

'Do you have to leave?' Julie asked Cider as the stragglers passed. She seemed genuinely disappointed; she must have found it unusual to be getting some real, unqualified attention, as opposed to shining only with the reflected light of Bruce McBride.

'Pretty lady, when I hear the siren's call I can't hold back. Tonight I'm dancing.'

'But that's tonight. It's barely three-thirty now.'

'Don't leave me much time, do it? I got preparations to make.'

'When you're as ugly as this guy,' Nick explained helpfully, 'you need all the time you can manage.'

'Ignore this hick, he's got two left feet. Good job he rides a bike with his backside, because that's where his brains are. When Cider Jones prepares, Notting Hill turns out and stares.'

'Notting Hill?' Julie said. 'Where?'

'North-west London,' Nick told her.

'Little place that's kind of like home,' Cider added.

'I know it. I meant which place in Notting Hill.'

'Sapphire Club,' Cider said. 'Carnival time tonight. You sure you want to be a doctor? Think of all the living you could be doing instead. It could take years and years– you'll be an old maid with one of those listening things around your neck.'

'A stethoscope?'

'I thought he was one of them Greek singers.'

She laughed. 'Maybe we can join you later.'

'You may have to. The way things go on Saturday nights, everything starts to come apart.'

They almost missed what happened next. None of them was really looking towards the track, but an instantaneous wave of tension swept through the crowd as the fast passage of the angry-sounding bikes became a tangle and then a knot. Two of them banged together hard and went over, one rider coming off straight away and the other – it looked like Le Fours in his distinctive red and white leathers – staying with the machines for a second or so, before being bowled clear and out onto the open track in the path of the following bikes.

Evans wobbled and lost speed, as he made a fast correction to avoid the sliding body, but his new course guided him into the rolling machines. He tried to turn again and he almost came clear but his back wheel snagged and flipped him around and off. The crack as his helmet banged onto the ground was audible right across the stands, even over the roar of the bikes and the urgent excitement of the commentary.

It was over in less than five seconds. Stoddard came through with no trouble, but McBride, Nichols and Mendoza were now clear ahead in a close group; Trans-World were going to take the first three places, real headline-grabbing stuff. Such were the speeds on the track that they were well away before the consequences of their barricading techniques could be felt.

The ambulance was on its way to the inner curve and stewards were already hauling one of the bikes clear, as the other riders came through behind Stoddard. None seemed to hesitate, or look back, or even slow down; their eyes and minds were filled with the demands of the race, and there was no room for compassion or concern. Not now, not on the track.

Dennison had righted his bike and was attempting to get back into the race. The fairing around his machine had cracked but had also protected the frame from damage as it absorbed the shock of impact; he'd lost a lot of time and the end of the race was near, but he still managed to accelerate into a place before the last man, and hold it as he leaned into the approaching curve.

Evans was standing but shaky, and the two ambulancemen had little difficulty in persuading him to subside onto a stretcher. Le Fours was angry and taking it out on the stewards; if he got any more agitated it seemed likely he'd take a swing at one or the other of them as they tried to placate him. He turned abruptly and walked away, back towards the pits.

'I think they're all okay,' Nick reassured Julie. After a racing pile-up, if you weren't actually dead you were considered to be okay. Most crash injuries would heal, and what wouldn't heal could be strapped or pinned or simply endured so that the next race need not be missed.

The race was more like a procession after that. The three Suzukis maintained their lead over the rest of the field and there were only a few changes in the order further back. Stoddard was passed twice, and Dennison managed to make up one place, before having to drop out altogether, as his machine managed to register its protests at the treatment it had received. Le Fours was still walking along the inner verge of the track, wrapped up in his own frustration and misery; with his helmet off, he proved to be a slight young man with long blond hair, that had been pressed into a limp shock. He didn't look up as the Trans-World team passed in close formation, but he spat on the grass.

After thirteen laps the chequered flag was being shaken out and made ready. The result had been obvious for some time, but there was still an enthusiastic response from the crowd as McBride crossed the line for what the course commentary said was his eighth Formula 750 win of the season. McBride responded to the cheers and applause of the crowd by throwing a wheelie, the heavy bike rearing dangerously and proud for thirty yards or more before the leading wheel dropped back to the ground. Typical bragging McBride showmanship, Nick thought, the idea not entirely untinged by envy. He gave a few polite claps for

Julie's sake – he'd already earned more of her disapproval than he really wanted – but Cider applauded with real enthusiasm.

'Want to go down?' Julie said to Cider and Nick. 'You could shake his hand.'

Nick didn't want a reconciliation and McBride probably didn't think he rated one, but obviously he wasn't going to say so. Julie led the way down from the stand, where Cider left them.

'Listen, Nick,' he said while Julie couldn't hear, 'don't overplay this. It's not only bikes you can burn up by trying too hard, okay?'

Nick grinned and slapped him on the shoulder. 'Don't worry,' he said.

When McBride had completed his victory lap he rolled into the pits and was immediately surrounded by the operatives of the Trans-World backup team, their numbers holding back, for a moment, the ranks of journalists and well-wishers. Peterson was in first, clearing the area immediately around the bike so that the team's Press Officer could bring the photographers in; McBride held his pose – and his smile – for as long as they needed to get their shots. As soon as he dismounted two mechanics reached in and wheeled the bike away, almost as if it were a Countess's necklace being returned to the vaults immediately after the latest State occasion.

Peterson moved in as soon as the initial scramble was over. He shook McBride's hand as they moved into the open-ended garage that was the Trans-World pit, but it was a perfunctory gesture; winning was to be expected, not something remarkable. 'Doesn't affect your world placing,' he said, 'but it's five thousand dollars.'

McBride was unaffected. He hadn't paid a bill or signed a personal cheque in three years or more, and he was indifferent to money in a way that only those who have no

Nick Freeman.

His bids for fame and fortune . . .

. . . always seemed to end one way.

Then tragedy struck.

But Greg's death . . .

. . . gave Nick his first big chance.

The Silver Dream Racer.

The chance for revenge . . .

. . . and for Julie . . .

. . . and for victory.

But what would be the cost?

lack of it can achieve. 'How was my time?' he said, pressing for what really interested him.

'One half-second short of the lap record.'

'Was that on lap nine?'

'That was the one, right after the pile-up when you went off on your own.'

'There was oil on the hill from lap ten on. I didn't risk it.'

'Dennison's bike probably dropped it. The damn fool tried to mount up and get back in the race, but his machine cut out on him after one trip around.'

'That's probably it. I didn't try to push things. I had a decent enough lead by then.'

'That's right. Save it for the big one.'

The big one was, of course, the British Grand Prix at Silverstone. It seemed to remind McBride of something. 'Hey,' he said, 'did you check on that bike?'

'Look, Bruce,' Peterson said patiently, 'forget the bike for now. The guy's a no-account privateer and we have a crowded schedule. You want to chase something like that, do it after the end of the season when there's some slack time.'

McBride began a half-hearted protest, knowing that when Peterson was firm he was immovable, but the sound of Julie calling his name distracted him. He saw her pushing through the crowd and feigned near-collapse, shouting, 'Medic, fast, I'm dying!'

Julie giggled as he hugged her. It was exuberant and showy, like everything he did. 'Thank god you're here,' he said. 'I need someone to walk down my spine.'

'There's nothing wrong with your body except that your head's attached to it. I can fix that if you really want me to.'

'What kind of procedure do you call that?'

'Some half-witted researcher back in the States does it

all the time with monkeys. I reckon it's no more than a short step from a monkey to a McBride.'

'You're saying I need a body transplant?'

'That's the one thing you don't need.'

'Stop boosting him up!' Peterson pleaded. 'Every time he wins a penny-ante race, Trans-World gets stuck with a paternity suit.'

'Come on, Al. If you won't let me drink and you count all my calories, how else am I supposed to celebrate? And anyway, what's all this penny-ante stuff? There were some good guys out there today.'

'You're only saying that,' Julie told him, 'to make your win sound better.'

'Al?' McBride said as they moved towards the gate which led out of the pits. 'Al, you're supposed to run this outfit. Do I have to tolerate that from a member of the audience?'

'Shut up and take it,' Peterson said. 'It's doing you good.'

The inevitable gang of youths and children were waiting at the gate in the chainlink screen that marked the division between the pits and the public part of the course. As McBride came near they began to wave their autograph books and programmes in the hope that he would come over and sign them. This was a PR job for which he needed no urging. Julie looked around for Nick, but he'd somehow drifted back in the crowd.

'Not riding today, then?' Nick looked around to see Pete Stoddard. His race leathers were unzipped and his shirt was damp and plastered to his skin.

'Not me. Not today.'

'Bike problem again?'

Nick shook his head. 'Money problem again.'

'Ah,' Stoddard said knowingly. 'The big M. I sold my kids last week to raise today's starting money. Wish I hadn't bothered.'

'You got a bad break. I saw how that spill slowed you up.'

'Yeah, well . . . I could tell you a thing or two about that ride.' Stoddard was looking over to where the Trans-World mechanics were loading their spares and equipment into the back of one of their glittering vehicles. 'Still, there's other chances coming up. Know anyone who wants to buy a mother-in-law?'

'You expect someone to pay *you*? Listen, I want to ask you something. Say you got your hands on a brand-new bike, some fantastic one-off—'

'Give me half a chance . . .'

'Yeah, well, say you had the chance, where would you go for cash?'

Stoddard thought for a moment. 'You mean for spares, someone to look after it, that kind of thing?' Nick nodded. 'Couldn't really say offhand, but I know I'd get it, even if I had to sell myself in bits to an organ bank. If you're really keen, you'll find a way. Like selling your mother-in-law.'

'Thanks, Pete,' Nick said, 'you're a great help.'

'If it was good enough, I should think one of the big companies would want it, obviously. EMW are always looking for new ideas, aren't they?'

'I want to ride it, not sell it.'

Somebody was calling to Stoddard, and he waved to show that he'd heard. 'Look,' he told Nick confidentially, 'wait until there's not so many people around. Then I'll tell you *my* fantasy.'

He was called again, so he said a grinning goodbye and moved off. As Nick turned he came face to face with Julie, who said, 'Where'd you get to?'

'I met a friend. I was just coming over.'

'Not much point now that everyone's gone. But listen,

there's some sort of reception tonight. Al Peterson should be there.'

'Is that good?'

'Not if you consider owning Trans-World to be bad. You could get his advice on that bike of yours.'

'I'm not selling it.'

'Nobody's talking about selling it. You don't have to get into anything you don't like, but Peterson's been in the business longer than anyone I know, and he talks a lot of sense. It won't hurt you just to listen, will it?'

'I suppose not.'

'Bruce's hotel at nine o'clock. Think you can make it?'

Nick glanced at his watch, and seemed to make up his mind. 'I'll start walking now,' he said.

TEN

She offered him a lift back into London, as he'd known she would. The roads were jammed with traffic after the meeting and the local police had diversions in operation, so it was half an hour or more before they were set on a straight course for home. Darkness fell as they travelled, and as they came to the city, streetlights and shopfronts flared in electric anticipation of the night.

'I know it's none of my business,' Nick said, 'but I had you two figured for a unit, if you see what I mean.'

The white MG shook as the tyres bounced over the kerb on a tight corner, and a couple of pedestrians scattered. Nick smiled pleasantly and hoped that the perspiration on his forehead wasn't too obvious. He wasn't a good passenger at the best of times, and Julie seemed to have had her training on fairground dodgems.

'Unit?' she said, obviously amused. 'Anybody ever tell you, you have a quaint turn of phrase? I'm Godmother to his two little girls!'

This was good news to Nick. He savoured it for a moment, and actually began to relax a little. 'Where are you studying?' he said after a while.

'St Thomas' Hospital. Does that count against me too?'

'For how long?'

'A year. Starting in the Fall.'

Nick nodded, and seemed pleased. 'Long enough.'

'Long enough for what?'

He shrugged, and smiled again. 'Anything,' he said.

She laughed, and did a fast gearchange that wasn't really called for. The engine howled in protest and a horn blared behind as a large saloon swung away out of danger. She didn't seem to be aware that anything was wrong.

'How long have you been driving this?' Nick ventured, indicating the car.

'Three days. Why?'

He was tempted to ask if those three days represented her entire driving experience, but all he could manage was, 'Nice car . . .'

'It should be,' she said, missing the point entirely. 'Cost me almost everything I have.'

'Yeah,' Nick said glassily. 'Try to hang on to it.'

They pulled into a garage forecourt at his direction. Carol would be home by now, and if she saw them she might get the wrong idea. Even worse, she might get the *right* idea.

'Thanks,' he said, relieved to feel solid concrete under him. He put a hand on the side of the car and waited for the world to steady up. Julie looked across at him from the driver's seat. 'See you later,' he told her.

'You live near here?'

'Along the road, just a block.'

'You ashamed of me, or something?'

'The neighbourhood's sort of . . . well, it's not what you're used to.'

'Listen,' she said, and there was a knowing look in her eyes that told Nick she understood more than he'd felt able to say, 'you don't have to explain because I've been through it all myself. The reception's at the Royal Garden Hotel – you know it?' Nick nodded as he thought of the imposing Chelsea structure. 'Be there about nine, with a friend if you want. Okay?'

With that, she let in the clutch noisily. The MG abruptly threw itself across the forecourt and nosed, without warning, into the passing traffic. There was a flurry of squealing brakes and angry hoots. Nick watched her red tail lights

94

until they were swallowed by the traffic. He was no longer sure of his attitude towards her; every time he had a neat compartment worked out in his mind she changed his ideas, from McBride's mistress to Jimmy Prince's widow to – what? Was her interest in Nick and the Silver Dream no more than the result of another misreading of her character?

It was Saturday night, and there was energy in the air. An early-evening drunk rummaged unsteadily through a stack of rubbish bags that had been heaped black and shiny against a boarded shopfront, roaring something incomprehensible to himself as he searched. As Nick passed, a Jamaican woman was berating the drunk in an accent as rich as butter, but still he mumbled and sifted.

The light was on in the hall when Nick stepped through the front door, bright on the red and cream gloss of the walls. He was hit by a sickly sweet odour; the two teenage Buonaguidi boys were lounging just inside, propped against opposite walls with an overdressed giggling girl each. They were passing a joint across, weaving unsteadily and talking too loudly in that hip Italian-American accent they'd picked up from the TV and which Nick could never understand.

One of them recognized him through the bilious haze and called his name, waving the joint at him. Nick muttered something to placate the boy as he pushed through and fumbled in his pocket for his key, and as he turned into the stairs the Buonaguidi boys laughed and the girls giggled.

Nick turned as a door off the stairs opened without warning and the sounds of a TV quiz show filtered into the hall. A careworn woman in late middle age, her face drawn and lined by worry and her greying hair pulled back under a knotted scarf, was bearing down on him.

'Hey,' she said, 'why don't you tell me, huh?'

'Tell you what?' Nick was puzzled; her sudden appearance suggested that she'd been listening for him.

'A month.' She thrust out an upturned palm and glared at him. 'I wanna month.'

Oh shit, he thought, her mind's going. 'I paid you Monday,' he told her, raising his voice in the hope that it might help understanding. 'Don't you remember?'

She shook her head firmly. 'Deposit,' she said. 'When you come, you never pay deposit. I tell you okay, you pay when you leave. I wanna month.'

'But I'm not leaving.'

'Is one month.'

'I am not leaving, Mrs Buonaguidi!' Nick laid it on heavy, his exasperation showing. The woman stared blankly at him for a moment, and then understanding seemed to dawn. Her eyes narrowed and a half-knowing smile spread across her face.

'Oh,' she said, nodding and backing towards the open doorway. 'Okay. Is okay.'

'Yeah,' Nick muttered to himself as he carried on up the stairs, 'and old-a cow is old-a cow.'

The door behind him slammed with a force that suggested she'd caught his tone if not the words, but he was too tired even to be pleased. He'd been up and around since five, and maybe he'd best sprawl on the sofa for a couple of hours before digging out his funeral suit and trying to make himself presentable for the reception. He hadn't yet thought how he would explain it to Carol.

There were no lights when he stepped into the flat, but already he knew that something was wrong; his footsteps and breathing had an indefinable echo, a hard edge that suggested that things were not as they should be. He reached for the lightswitch and flicked it on.

The room was immediately bathed with the harsh light of a naked bulb. Not only had the shade been removed, but the furniture was stripped down to the bare essentials; the coffee-tables and the bookcases that Carol had bought from the store on staff discount had gone. So had the stereo, and the posters on the walls, pale rectangles and pinholes showing on the wallpaper where they'd been. The creaking sofa remained, and the cheap kitchen chairs that belonged to the landlord, but even the plants had been taken.

It was the same in the bedroom. The bed was stripped down to the bare mattress, unashamedly showing its rips and stains to the world, and one side of the massive Victorian wardrobe stood open. Everything of Carol's had been removed, every item she'd bought whilst his money had gone on his bikes and racing. Christ, he thought, she must have had a lorry round this afternoon to shift it all so fast. So this is what the old woman was so concerned about – she thought we were skipping out on her.

He found the phone in the sitting room perched on a pile of old magazines. He pushed them over and threw them around as he looked for the directory. The book had passed through the hands of a number of earlier tenants and each had added a few doodles and hastily-noted numbers, until the cover was a forest of graffiti. It took Nick a few moments to find the number that he wanted, and then he dialed and waited.

'Hello, Linda?' he said as the receiver was lifted, 'It's Nick. I was wondering if—' Linda, sounding rather defensive, wanted to know Nick who. 'Nick Freeman. I was wondering if—' Linda wanted to know how he was. 'I'm fine. Listen, is Carol with you?' There was a hurried consultation at the other end of the line, the conclusion of which was that Carol wasn't. 'Any idea how I could get in touch with her?' Linda didn't actually know, and why didn't he try her folks? 'But her folks live in Ireland—' Now Linda's doorbell was ringing and it was nice to talk to you, Nick, 'bye. 'Hey, hold on,' Nick said, 'I want the number . . . Linda?' But Linda, like Carol, had quietly slipped away.

He slammed the receiver down. 'Thanks, Linda,' he said. 'Up yours, Linda.' Then he pushed himself to his feet and walked to the door.

As soon as Bruce McBride had found out that Simon Addison had never actually written anything derogatory about him that was it, inner-sanctum time. Addison was allowed to join the select group who sat around him and were on the receiving end of his views on life in general and racing and winning in particular. Modesty had never been one of McBride's weaknesses.

They'd pulled a few chairs together to make an impromptu auditorium at one side of the high-ceilinged convention room, to which spot the girls in the short skirts and the Trans-World sashes who carried around the champagne trays had made more visits than to anywhere else in the room. On the other side of the buffet table Nichols and Mendoza had managed to marshall their own audience of admirers, and were keeping them highly amused with a routine that they'd used at innumerable similar gatherings. It involved Mendoza making endless preparations to balance a glass of champagne on his head, whilst Clarke Nichols harangued and challenged him; they could keep it up for an hour or more, building anticipation with a mastery that belied long rehearsal. In the end when the time was right, one or another of them would be drenched in champagne, which would be a good line to move the party upstairs to one of their suites, whilst the grinning victim showered and changed, usually in company.

Julie was on the edge of McBride's crowd. She'd heard most of it before, so she was only half-listening. A couple of times she glanced at the electric clock over the bar and then at the door. Addison was sitting the closest to McBride, and he was swaying slightly; the only effect that the drink seemed to be having on McBride himself was that it made him talk louder and faster.

'Listen,' he was saying, and Addison was nodding profoundly, 'you can talk in clichés about exhilaration but it's more. Why do guys climb Everest when they could sit at home and watch TV? There it is, the big D – cheat death and you live higher, that's what Jimmy Prince always used to say, right, Julie?' Julie gave a brief smile of confirmation, but he wasn't even looking at her. 'Jimmy Prince lived higher than any man I knew. I mean, that has to be some philosophy.'

She drifted away from the group towards the spot where she could see Al Peterson would shortly be free. He was wrapping up a conversation with a couple of grinning Suzuki executives, and she slipped in neatly to put a hand on his arm, as he turned away, still wearing his public-relations smile.

'Al,' she said, 'have you got a minute?'

'Apart from the merchandising people waiting in the lobby, the exclusive for Time-Life, and four calls from Tokyo, I've got all night.' But he said it indulgently, making it obvious that he always had time for Julie.

'Okay, short and sweet. You once said to come to you if I needed help, financial advice, anything like that, right?'

'Sure. What's the problem?'

'It's no problem. I think I might act like a catalyst and do two people a favour.'

'Anyone I know?'

'One of them is someone I just met today. The other one is you.'

'I'm all ears,' he said, although his smile was more good-natured than anything else. He didn't really believe that she was going to come up with anything that would overturn his world, but he wasn't going to be unkind enough to say so. Julie led him a little further away from McBride's group, which was starting to get a little more noisy.

'How long is it,' she said, 'since the basic design of a motorcycle, any motorcycle, could be described as revolutionary?'

'Revolutionary? You mean improvements, modifications, anything like that?'

'Not just modifications. Basic design.'

'*Basic* design? Well, there's been nothing you could call basic been changed since the first motorcycle. You rig a frame, you bolt an engine to it, and you hang a wheel on either end. It doesn't leave you much to play around with.'

She was looking in her purse. She took out a folded piece of typewritten paper, the specifications sheet that Nick had shown her in the Brands Hatch grandstand and which she'd neglected to give back. She smoothed it out and handed it over. 'I saw that machine on the track before practice this morning. The guy who owns it doesn't have a cent to his name and he's going to walk through that door any minute. Will you talk to him?'

Peterson was shaking his head, world-weary, as he looked at the sheet, trying to choose his words in a way that would not offend her. 'Julie, is this the bike Bruce saw?'

'That's the one.'

'Look, Julie, there are bike nuts all over the world with this kind of thing in the garage. Most of them will never even run.'

'This one runs. Runs pretty well, and it looks good too.'

'Looking good doesn't make a good machine.'

'Al, I'm not asking you to buy in or anything like that. All I'm asking is, will you talk to this guy? He needs advice on how to handle it. He's never been into anything this big before.'

'Of course I will,' Peterson relented. 'I'll talk to him.'

The doorman at the Sapphire Club almost turned Nick around and propelled him back into the street before he could speak, but the mention of Cider Jones' name was enough to mollify him even if it didn't actually make him happy. The doorman was a glowing ebony giant in an overstretched evening jacket, and he looked at Nick narrowly. 'You wanna go in *there*?' he said, and when Nick nodded the doorman shrugged. 'Your life, brother,' he said, and sent him to the cash booth where the same procedure was repeated.

Nick got a couple of disbelieving looks from people he passed in the paint-peeling corridor, on his way downstairs to where the music was loudest. The Sapphire was an exclusively black disco, and Nick knew that he was risking antagonism; once inside he'd have to find Cider, and fast.

The music seemed to have been boosted by several decibels as he emerged from the stairway and looked down into the club. The dance-floor was brightly lit in raw moving colours but all around was muted and dim, the only other focus of light being behind the bar. None of the dancing figures was Cider, and Nick didn't want to risk moving among the tables looking at the faces, for fear of providing an easy excuse for misinterpretation and aggression. He descended the last few steps and moved towards the bar.

There were a few startled looks as he pushed his way through, and a hand fell on his shoulder. He turned sharply, expecting the worst.

'Hey, Nick!' It was Cider's elder brother, the enigmatically-named Face, and he was shouting to make himself heard over the music. 'You can't come in here without an escort, you'll get lynched!'

'Fuck all that,' Nick said with the determination that had made him heedless, 'I'm looking for your brother.'

'Well, he ain't here. We just had the dance competition and *I* won.'

'Shit,' said Nick with a frown.

'That's no way to treat success,' Face said, pretending to be offended.

'He said he was definitely coming.'

'That's Cider for you, all talk and no performance. Want me to chaperone you to the bar?'

They started to move towards the lights, and conversation became slightly easier. Nick pulled out a handful of change – all the money that he had left after being rooked at the door – and said, 'You don't drink Bloody Marys, do you?'

'The whole family does, man.'

'Shit. Where's the phone?'

At the Royal Garden Hotel the party was moving into its depressed phase. The drinks were getting scarce and the air was getting stale: the canapes no longer circulated and the buffet table was a vast emptiness dotted with crumbs and half-bitten vol-au-vents. The smiles on the faces of the short-skirted Trans-World girls had become noticeably fixed and glassy, as they moved around picking up empty glasses, misted as if with a film of dried soap. Only Bruce McBride's energies seemed undiminished, but he was employing them on a considerably reduced audience.

Simon Addison had seen Julie sitting a little apart from the group and had swayed over to bring her some company and comfort. She had to move her chair so that she could still see the door, but Addison didn't seem to notice and only hitched his own chair nearer. He was trying to get together a short feature, he explained, built around what McBride had said about cheating death and living higher, and didn't she think this was kind of a unique philosophy?

'Unique is right,' she said. 'Uniquely dangerous. Do you know how many riders die each year?'

'Bet you the public know,' Addison said, 'because they carry on packing the stands at every meeting, don't they?'

Suddenly she was no longer looking towards the door; she was looking at Addison, her eyes were hard and there was a note of wary aggression in her voice. 'Are you saying that's why they come?'

She'd cut through the conversation of the adjacent group, and McBride leaned over and touched her arm. 'No, hold it, Julie,' he warned with unusual diplomacy whilst Addison blinked in surprise at the reaction he'd evoked. 'He didn't say that.'

Julie ignored him. 'So what *are* you saying? Twenty million ghouls turn out each year hoping to see two dozen guys smash their heads into pulp?'

Addison opened his mouth to answer but suddenly Al Peterson was between them. He'd had a tough night of it and he was obviously tired. He asked the rest of the group to excuse him and then leaned in to speak to Julie. 'Listen,' he said, 'I can't wait any longer. If your man wants to talk, have him call me tomorrow, okay?'

She smiled and nodded; Peterson had hung around for longer than he really wanted already. He said goodnight to everyone, and moved away.

McBride looked after him, an expression of puzzled enquiry on his face. 'Have who call him tomorrow?' he said.

'I wouldn't mind so much,' Nick said, sipping at his

103

Bloody Mary and wincing at the unaccustomed flavour, 'if she'd left me a note or something. Why couldn't she leave a note?'

Face gazed across the bar to the dance-floor where the colours pulsed and the music was deep and loud. 'Maybe she can't write,' he said.

'It's crazy. I mean, you and Cider dance. It's your thing . . . do it all the time, right? The two of you.' Christ, he thought, three of these disgusting cocktails and I can hardly get my words together. Either I'm tired or there's more in them than I thought.

'We dance, but we do it separately,' Face corrected. 'But go on.'

'Well, I ride bikes. Now, do girls avoid you because you dance? I mean, do they?'

Face smirked and raised his eyebrows. 'Not because I dance,' he said.

'So why do I get dumped on just because I ride a damn bike?' Nick broke off for a moment to crane his neck and look towards the telephone at the end of the bar. The queue had dropped to one.

'Just one of the mysteries of the universe,' Face said profoundly.

'Okay, so it's dangerous. But so's mending a fuse.'

'Hey, did you explain that to Carol? I mean just come straight out with it, honey, it's like mending a fuse?'

'You're as bad as your brother, you know that?'

'Man, I'm worse. I been practising longer.'

'But, I mean . . . what's wrong with them? Women? What is *wrong* with them.'

'Are you kidding?' Face said with a pained expression. 'I'm a fag.'

But Nick was in full spate and deaf to minor objections. 'What's wrong with women is . . .' he hesitated, on the brink of great discovery. 'Well . . . there's something missing, know what I mean? They don't have . . . oh, I don't know . . .'

'Balls?' supplied Face.

Nick was about to reply when he saw that the phone was at last free. In the corner of his eye he could also see that somebody was moving across the bar towards it, so he slapped down his drink and got there first. It was difficult to read the number scratched in biro on the back of his hand and on the first attempt he mis-dialled, but the next time he got through to the Royal Garden switchboard and asked for room five-fifteen. Leave a message there, Julie had told him, and it'll get to me.

McBride caught up with Julie in the fifth-floor corridor, just as the downward elevator doors were closing. Back in the convention room a telephone was ringing behind the bar, distant and shrill, but the shutters were down and the staff were busy clearing tables and loading trolleys with soiled linen and crockery.

'I'm waiting, Julie,' McBride said.

'For what?' she said, genuinely uncomprehending. She touched the '*call*' button for the next elevator down, and it glowed with a promise of service.

'Let's get one thing straight. The guy's a creep. If Al can do a deal for the bike, then okay. Maybe with Suzuki I could develop it, but that Freeman guy's a loser and a creep. Any deal for him personally is out.'

'Hey, stop!' Julie said. 'Who's talking about Suzuki? Or you, for that matter?'

'You said he was interested in a deal.'

'I said he's going to talk to Al. He wants advice, that's all.'

A discreet *ping* announced the arrival of the elevator,

and the glowing call button winked out as the doors slid apart.

'Listen,' McBride said as they stepped from the ambers and browns of the hotel corridor to the amber and brown of the empty elevator. 'I don't even want him talking until I've had a chance to get the bike analysed and tested it myself. Al does no deal unless that machine is for me and me alone, okay?' Julie touched the foyer button, and the doors whispered closed. 'It's simple sense,' McBride went on. 'There's no room on the team for all that chip-on-shoulder, self-pitying shit – even if the guy was good, which he's not. You should know that if anybody does.'

She'd resisted rising, but now she turned to him with a fire in her eyes. 'Self-pity? Bruce, I'm going to say something to you.' There was something in her manner that made him defensive, but he was effectively trapped in the descending car. He looked up at the indicator board; the number four winked out, the number three lit up.

'Last year in Colorado,' she said slowly, 'you came to me in tears. Jimmy was dead and it was *your fault*.'

'Stop it, Julie,' he said quietly, but there was no way she'd be stopped now.

'You wished you'd never come to Europe for the season. You were never going to go again. You were going to give up riding, go back to law school – I never saw so much self-pity in my whole *life*!'

McBride exploded without warning. He grabbed her by the arms and slung her hard into the corner of the car and the whole car shook as they passed the second floor. 'Didn't keep you out of my bed, did it?' he roared, his face only inches from hers. 'Last year in Colorado, you got what you wanted and now you're back for *more*!'

She tried to push him away, but he caught her hand easily and threw it aside. His fury was distorted by her tears of anger and fear. 'What are you trying to say?'

'What the hell do you think I'm saying? The truth, damn it, you wanted him dead and you got him dead. Didn't mourn long, did you?'

The car eased to a halt and the doors began to slide. She saw freedom and tried to dart for it, but McBride caught her arm.

'Julie, wait,' he said, getting himself back under control for the benefit of the bemused faces that turned to them in the lobby, but Julie wasn't about to give him any help in managing his image.

'Get your hands off me,' she said, and then she pulled free and ran down the lobby. Heads turned as McBride strode after her, through the revolving door and out into the night.

He caught up with her before she could reach her MG. 'Julie, stop this.'

She whirled on him, almost shouting. 'I tried to take a whole bottle of Valium. I was so guilty about you I almost lost my mind.'

Pity you weren't serious enough to make the gesture successful, he thought, but all he said was, 'Shut up, will you?'

'When I woke up that morning, you were smiling. Your greatest rival was dead, you were in bed with his widow and you were *smiling*!'

'Will you shut up?'

'Well, smile while you can, 'cause I'm going to wipe that smile clean off your face.' With a savage burst of energy that would probably leave bruises on her arm she pulled away from him and walked off into the night.

'What with?' he shouted after her in fury. 'What *with*?'

ELEVEN

People came out of the Sapphire Club in curiosity at the roaring of the motorcycle in the alley outside. It could be heard in the corridor, and the word spread quickly; it was Saturday night, when anything unusual and off-beat guaranteed an audience.

The watchers were swelled by numbers from the other clubs and dives which traded off the car-choked Notting Hill alley, and soon there was a good crowd to applaud and whistle as the young and tousle-haired lunatic on the high-powered bike made yet another speedway turn around the parked vehicles, fighting the leading wheel and spraying grit as he went. Then he was lined up and gunning the motor to come stampeding back down the open space in the centre of the cul-de-sac, the note building higher and higher until he let out the clutch with a scream of whirling rubber on tarmac and hurtled forward, jamming his weight back in the saddle and hauling on the bars, to rear into a high wheelie.

The bike scooted down the alley on its back wheel, before slamming down hard and roaring into a sideways slide, which brought Nick up just a couple of feet short of the brick wall at the road's end. Under the Sapphire Club's neon sign his original audience of half a dozen leather-and-studs youths and girls were standing by their bikes and cheering.

'Who's the idiot?' one of the girls, a late-comer, asked.

'Acid freak,' one of her friends told her. 'Gotta be.'

Nick had laid the bike into a tight U-turn between two cars, bouncing up onto the kerb and then back onto the road again, pulling around straight and pouring in the power for another wheelie. There was another derisive cheer as he passed the group, the bike teetering dangerously, and then he had to swerve hard to avoid the white MG that was pulling without warning into the alley. There was a chorus of protest from this car and from the one behind it which had braked suddenly. Nick turned again and streaked back, cutting savagely in front of the MG, and slammed to a halt outside the Sapphire. The leather-and-studs gang seemed to be disappointed that he hadn't actually fallen off, but Nick seemed insensitive to their mockery; he swayed off the bike and said, 'Well?'

One of the youths came forward as Nick stood there beaming in self-satisfaction. The youth's girlfriend was scowling and tugging at his arm, but he seemed prepared to admit that a bet was a bet. He counted out three notes into Nick's outstretched hand. Nick was still supporting the weight of the bike – or was it the bike supporting him? – as he stuffed the money into his pocket and said, 'Want to bet me on a seven-fifty?'

The youth was starting to reply when Nick's world abruptly exploded into bright lights. When the bells and the starbursts had died down a little he found that his nose was bleeding and he was looking up at a fifteen-foot giant with a face like thunder.

'Next time you want to ride my bike,' the giant rumbled, 'you can ask me first!'

He bent and took a good double-handful of the front of Nick's jacket and hauled him to his feet. Off the floor and with the rattling in his head only slightly diminished Nick could see that the giant wasn't really fifteen feet tall, perhaps a more manageable seven or eight. His anger was just as fierce no matter what angle you saw it from. A couple of his friends – less than giants, just plain, honest unholy thugs – were lifting the bike from where it had fallen.

'Get up!' he said as Nick subsided to the floor without support. 'Come on, get up!'

Nick made it to his feet and the big man knocked him down again, the ground rushing up to meet him and smacking all the wind out of him. Then the giant planted a kick which shook his ribcage and made him want to throw up, and the Bloody Mary fog was driven from his mind as Nick tasted real blood and his own bile.

He contrived to get half-up and to dodge the giant's next blow, but it was more through luck than through good footwork, because the world was still only half in focus, flaring lights spinning before him against the dark, blurred faces and a distant, tinny sound of voices. The bastards were cheering the fight just as they'd cheered his riding.

Okay, he thought, this is it: Freeman strikes back. He raised his fist and swung for where he estimated the giant to be, missing completely and putting a sizeable dent in the door of a nearby car; the pain didn't start until a few seconds later, after the bike-owning ogre had given him another hard bang on the side of the head and sent him spinning backwards.

Nick sprawled on the pavement with his hand on fire and one eye near to closing. A white angel bent and reached for him; Jesus, he thought, am I as badly hurt as *that*? The angel swam into close focus and became Julie Prince in a white evening gown, concern on her face. Behind her was the leather-and-studs youth with a small dose of guilt showing through his glee. 'It wasn't actually my bike,' the youth explained unnecessarily, and Julie said, 'Nick! Are you all right?'

A brief respite from the battering, and Nick was starting to get back his grip on the world. The giant had turned away; he could see over Julie's shoulder that the big man was bending to inspect his machine for damage. Nick started to yell defiantly and pushed Julie aside, boosting himself forward from her MG to catch the giant by his shoulder and spin him around to meet the swinging fist on the end of Nick's other arm. It landed square-on, smashing into the cheekbone and rocking the big man's head like a punchball on a chain as Nick jumped on him to follow through, getting in a couple more as they went down.

Now Nick had the upper hand and was laying in with enthusiasm, but within seconds the ogre's friends had come around and hauled Nick off, almost hitting each other in their keenness to damage him. Then the ogre was up and it was three onto one and Julie was shouting, but nobody around her was prepared to be anything more than a spectator. After all, it was Saturday night.

Suddenly there was action over by the Sapphire Club, and the crowd parted to let Face and a couple of friends through. Face took in the brutal tableau in a second and launched himself at a run, landing both feet in a high kick on the back of the ogre's neck. The ogre snapped forward as if he'd been hit by a shotgun blast and the two thugs were thrown apart as he cannoned into them. Face made a neat recovery in midair and landed two-footed and catlike, as Julie ran in to help Nick.

The ogre was up again, murder in his eyes, but now the numbers were even and the opponents were fresh, relaxed and capable. The thugs started to shuffle uneasily as the black smiled at them, tense and alert. Nick was on the floor and still fighting, but now even Julie was able to hold his arms down without too much trouble.

'You want to try out the National Health Service?' Face said, his voice silk-smooth and dangerous. 'Come a little closer . . .'

There was silence as the two sides watched each other. The giant and his thugs had found themselves in a situation they'd neither expected nor wanted, but there was no easy way that they could back out now. Julie had Nick back on his feet. He'd remembered where he was and he wanted to get back into the fight, but she was guiding him towards her car and he barely had the strength to resist.

A police siren sounded a couple of blocks away, and the silence was shattered. The thugs broke ranks and tried to scatter, and Face shot out a foot to trip the giant and send him sliding onto the tarmac. Nick saw his chance and pulled away from Julie, managing to get a kick in before she could catch his arm and pull him back. She bundled him into the MG without bothering to open the door and then ran around to slide into the driver's seat. The engine was still running and she banged the car into gear and made a tight turn into the cul-de-sac; as they swung past the Sapphire Club entrance Nick was waving both arms triumphantly over his head and threatening to fall out into the road.

'Where are we going?' he mumbled indistinctly as they moved out and lost themselves in the night traffic. She glanced sideways at him as if she were surprised that he could still speak.

'I'm taking you home,' she said. 'Believe it or not, that face needs looking at.'

For the second time that day she drove him home, this time taking him all the way to the flat instead of dumping him at the garage. During the ride his brain stopped singing from the battering and settled into a semblance of lucidity, so that he was able to give her adequate directions. He eased stiffly out of the car and shrugged off, as a matter of pride, her offer to help him up the steps to the front door.

The Buonaguidi boys had moved on with their giggling girls in tow, leaving only a sweetish odour in the stale hallway. As they stepped around the baby carriage Nick wondered if he should tell Julie about Carol; but then, he vaguely remembered saying something about it in the car, and anyway the broken hall light flicked off as he stood on the landing fumbling with his keys. He mumbled something then felt her hand on his in the dark; the keys were taken away and after a couple of seconds the door swung open and the room spilled its night and neon into the passageway.

He bounced into the low armchair. It bucked feebly and failed to throw him off. Julie went through into the kitchen and switched on the lights; he groaned as the brilliance stabbed into his eyes. She returned after a few minutes with a bowl of warm water and a half-bottle of disinfectant which she set on the floor beside him, and then she was gone again to return from the bathroom a few minutes later with a limp and raggedy-looking sponge.

'Not exactly Mount Sinai Medical,' she said, 'but it will have to do.' She fetched a standard lamp and set it close by; he tried to turn his face away but she took hold of his chin and gently guided it back, studying his injuries with an almost professional detachment. The skin around one eye was blue and swelling, and there was another hefty patch of bruising on his neck. His lip was split, more spectacular than serious, and the blood was drying in a dirty crust that would have to be washed off before sepsis could set in. Otherwise his bones seemed to hold him upright and his muscles stopped him from falling over. She pressed his ribs and got an angry grunt of protest in reply, but none of them was broken.

'I've seen it before,' she said as she soaked the sponge in the disinfectant solution and started to dab at the forming scab with firm pressure. 'It's some kind of deathwish.'

Nick squirmed and glowered as she worked; the help he could use, but the philosophy was decidedly unwelcome. She went on, 'Maybe I don't know you well enough to say this, but from what I've seen you're a walking disaster looking for some place to happen.'

She finished off and squeezed the bloody sponge out into the bowl, staining the water dark and red. She'd been careful in her work, but she hadn't spared him. 'Thanks,' he grunted, wincing at the effort and the pain of his lip, but he seemed less than grateful.

'Okay,' Julie said, making it obvious that he too was not exactly her number one favourite person in the world at the moment, 'I'll leave after I've said this one last thing. You stood me up. You made a fool out of me when I tried to help. Now that really pisses me off.' Nick was about to speak, but she stopped him. It wasn't difficult. 'Don't give me the line about how your girl moved out. If you treated her the way you seem to think you can treat me, I'm surprised she ever moved in.'

'Your patients are going to love you,' Nick croaked.

'Sure,' she said, taking the sarcasm in her stride, 'and I probably couldn't have fixed up the money for you anyhow. That saves you the trouble of saying it yourself.'

When she put it that way, he had to admit that he didn't come through the evening smelling of roses. 'Look,' he said as she looked for her evening purse, 'I'm sorry about tonight, really.'

From sarcasm to sincerity and he still failed to impress. 'Don't be,' she said. 'We'll both survive.'

'With your qualifications that won't be too difficult, will it?'

'Oh, fine. Go ahead, feel sorry for yourself. Feel sorry all you want, but do me one favour. Don't do it on my time.'

'*Your* time?' Nick said as he pushed himself up out of the chair to intercept her on her way to the door. 'This also happens to be *my* time. I didn't ask you to come up here and deliver a bloody lecture.'

'Can I say one last thing?'

'This'll be your second last thing.'

'Touché. Why aren't you happy?'

The question caught him unexpectedly, and he was lost for a quick and easy answer. 'Who says I'm not?' he said warily.

'You do. Your attitudes and your sour jokes, everything.'

He nodded. It hurt. 'Is the mercy mission over now?'

'Mercy mission?' she said, an eyebrow raised in unsmiling irony. 'Look on it as a kick in the ass.'

Arguing was no fun when you were sore and losing. Nick started to slump back into the chair. 'Okay, you've kicked it. Mind if I get some sleep?'

'You mean you're not asleep now?'

She was almost at the door before the remark penetrated. 'What's that supposed to mean?' he demanded with real annoyance, twisting around to call after her. She stopped and turned to face him.

'Who was it came on with all that bullshit about admiring Jimmy? About how you might have been world-class too, if you'd only had a chance? Who asked me to find a sponsor?' Her voice was rising in volume and losing its stability as emotion fed on anger. 'And who couldn't manage just one lousy phone-call to say that he wasn't going to make it? You're not fighting to end up on top of the pile. What you're doing is nothing better than jerking off.'

By now Nick was at the door, watching her with real interest. 'And what are you doing?' he said, and he wasn't making a retort; it was like she'd peeled back a whole new layer of reality for him, and he was slightly dazed by its wonder. 'I mean, why are you here? Medical Genius Saves Unknown Slob. It doesn't add up.'

'You're right,' she said, opening the door but not looking up at him. 'Good luck with your bike.'

He pushed the door, and she couldn't hold it. The lock snapped into place as it closed. 'Wait a minute,' he said, as understanding dawned, 'all this wouldn't have anything to do with a certain guy with sixty-four teeth, who thinks he can walk on water?'

Now she did look up, and her eyes were blazing. Nick was leaning on the door so she couldn't open it. 'I'm leaving now,' she said tightly, 'so would you mind letting—'

'Jackpot! It's Bruce McBride, isn't it?'

'Go to hell.'

'You don't have to say it,' Nick told her. He wasn't goading, he was really trying his hardest to get through and he realized that he hadn't had much practice. 'I was there. I watched it happen.'

'Will you get out of my way?'

'It was the oldest trick in the world.'

'*Please!*'

'One rider to win, and two to back him up. They single out the hottest contender, and box him in, one in front and one on the outside, get him really mad.'

She was covering her ears. 'I don't want to *hear* this!'

'Maybe you get him so mad that he kills himself. It's called legitimate tactics.'

All her defences were down and her control was stretched almost to its limit, but she still tried to pull away. 'Let me go,' she said. It was almost a plea.

'So now you're looking for someone to beat the hell out of Bruce McBride,' Nick said, and found the key which unlocked all her tears. She covered her face with her hands and began to slide down the wall, crumpling into a shapeless heap on the floor.

'Okay,' Nick said quietly as he bent to take her face in his hands. 'You've found him.'

TWELVE

The next morning Cider came into the hallway from the street and did a quick side-step shuffle to take him between the bicycle and the baby carriage. He was pleased with the manoeuvre and grinned broadly as he loped up the angled stairway towards Nick's door; as he turned the angle he could see Mrs Buonaguidi's scowling face protruding from the shadows.

'Morning,' he said, meeting her mute hostility with sweetness. 'Couldn't interest you in a secondhand bike, could I? TS five-hundred? Racing trim, good slicks?'

She pulled back sharply and closed the door. Cider shrugged. 'You'll change your mind when you see it,' he said, and turned to carry on up the stairs. Nick was blocking his way on the top step, leaning forward and supporting himself on the moulding overhead; behind him the door to the flat was open, showing the gaping emptiness of the room beyond.

'Shit!' Cider said in curious wonder, as his eyes came to rest on the rainbow hues of Nick's face, a sickly yellow, tingeing the blacks and the blues. 'What did they hit *you* with?'

Nick stabbed a finger at him. 'I want to talk to you,' he said, and turned to walk into the flat. Cider followed.

Once inside, he looked around and whistled appreciatively. 'Did a good job, didn't she?' he said.

'You knew?'

'My brother told me.'

'Yeah, that reminds me. Where *were* you last night?'

Cider dropped into the creaking armchair and slung his legs over the armrest. 'In the van.'

117

'Oh?' Nick said, amused at the idea. 'Who with?'

'Your damn bike, that's who.'

'You're putting me on.'

'Come on, man,' Cider said, rising to defend his own heroism, 'you know my neighbourhood.'

'You slept with it? All night? How'd you make out?'

Cider looked around at the stripped-out apartment and grinned. 'A whole lot better than you.'

'That's what I want to talk to you about. I need a favour.'

'What you really mean,' Cider said with a display of weariness, 'is that you need the van.'

'I know it's your turn, but today's special.'

Cider uncoiled himself from the chair and began to dig deep into his pocket for the keys. 'It always is,' he said, and then; 'Wait a minute – not McBride's girl?'

'That's right, she's not McBride's girl.'

Cider shook his head. 'Oh, man,' he said, dragging out the keys and throwing them over. 'Can you ever find trouble.'

Nick had told Cider that he was invited too, and Cider had asked where. Nick said they were going for a picnic on the Heath. Cider wanted to know when they'd fixed it up, and Nick admitted that he'd just thought of it.

There was a delicatessen just around the corner that opened on Sunday mornings, so they pooled their money and Cider went off to raid the stocks; whilst Nick phoned Julie and told her all about it. She sounded wary at first, as if the memories of her thoughts and impressions of the previous night were still unclear, but when she judged that Nick was friendly and relaxed, she unwound a little and said that it sounded like a great idea. She gave him directions of how to find her small flat – don't blink or you'll miss it – and he said that there was only one thing that she'd have to bring.

'What's that?' she said.

'Have you got a clean tablecloth? Somebody's pinched all mine.'

They parked the van on the outskirts of Highgate, not much more than a couple of blocks from the cemetery, and carried the food, Julie's cloth and mis-matched cutlery past the open water of the Highgate Ponds to Parliament Hill, from where they'd have a broad view of Hampstead Heath and the city beyond. There were bathers in the ponds and quite a few dogs and children romping on the grassy slopes.

But Cider wasn't with them for long. They were spreading the picnic out when two small children came sidling up, carrying a large and elaborate kite that they hadn't been able to get up into the air. Cider had the kind of radiant good nature that children and lost dogs always sensed from a distance, and he grinned when he saw them.

'Excuse me for a while,' he said to Julie and Nick. 'These are my kind of people.' And he went off to give them a hand with their kite.

When he'd gone, Julie asked Nick how he first got into racing, and Nick began telling her how it started with his teeange heroes – Mike Hailwood, Giacomo Agostini, Jimmy Prince . . . it was already out before he'd realized what he was saying.

'Sorry,' he said quickly, 'I suppose I'm on sensitive ground there, aren't I?'

'Oh, it's okay,' she told him. She spoke slowly and deliberately, as if she was telling him of ideas that she'd formed over a long period of time but which she'd never actually put into words before. 'I don't exactly like talking about it, but at least it's not unbearable any more. You know what does make it bearable?' She looked across at Nick. He was propped on one elbow, watching her closely.

'It's . . . well, if Jimmy had known that he was going to die that day, he would've gone out onto that track anyway. You know what I mean?'

'I know what you mean,' Nick told her. 'I understand. Completely.'

Julie shook her head. 'The great god, Speed.'

Nick levered himself up and reached across for a knife and a block of cheese. 'Yeah,' he said, 'it's the only show where the clowns pay to entertain the crowd.'

He cut an irregular chunk off the block – it was cheddar or Wensleydale, something bland and inoffensive – and she reached across and put her hand over his, while he was still holding the knife.

'Do you get migraine headaches?' she said.

'No,' Nick said, puzzled.

She took her hand away. 'Then you can have it.'

He looked at her blankly for a moment, and then they both laughed, together. Further down the hill Cider was charging along on the end of the kite-string, and the light-weight apparatus was bobbing along a few feet off the ground behind him, stubbornly refusing to soar. Cider feigned collapse at the end of the run, and the two children giggled and applauded as he tried weakly to struggle back to his feet.

Nick said, 'How long does it take to be a doctor?'

'Seven years.'

'Oh, dear,' he said with exaggerated solemnity. 'That's a long time.'

She raised her eyebrows and smiled as she tore a sweet roll to go with her own cheese. 'Well, what did you think it took? A couple of afternoons and a good memory?'

Cider was calling to her, struggling up the slope as if he barely had enough energy to stay upright. His hands and arms had become entangled in the strings of the stricken kite. A couple of loops had tied themselves over his head and he was tripping over the excess that trailed behind.

'Come on,' he gasped, 'you're a doctor. Try and cure this, will you?'

The string suddenly became taut and pulled his feet together, so that he pitched forward suddenly. The two children squealed with delight, and Julie was laughing as she went over to help get him untied.

Nick grinned to himself as he watched.

THIRTEEN

With Julie's encouragement Nick telephoned the bank early on the Monday morning. At eight-fifteen there was no reply and at eight-thirty he found himself talking to one of the cleaners, but at ten to nine he got hold of the Manager's Secretary and asked if it would be possible for him to have an early appointment. She asked him to hold on and then went off to spend a couple of minutes looking for the office diary. When she came back she told him Mr Hargreaves would be able to see him for ten minutes at nine-thirty. Nick thanked her and put the phone down, doing a quick mental calculation; there was no way he would make it to the garage before ten. Wiggins would come over, tapping his watch in a pantomime gesture and telling him all about the fire-breathing demons of the front office, but what the hell. He was half an hour late already.

Hargreaves was a middle-aged man with high cheek-bones and a face like a slab of cold meat. Nick had rehearsed his presentation in his mind, but the energy seemed to seep from it as he spread the documents and accounts on the desk, before this stony-faced being who had based a career on a lack of enthusiasm. His shirt was starched and his formal suit was devoid of style, as if he were ashamed of his body and determined to do nothing that might please it; Nick reckoned that his own suit was quite fashionable by comparison. Now he'd found two uses for it, funerals and high finance, and he wasn't sure which of the two he found the more intimidating.

Hargreaves listened, or to be more accurate he gave a poor imitation of listening. Nick struggled gamely on, and after exactly eight minutes Hargreaves cut in and said, 'Yes. Well . . . what exactly are you asking me to do?'

Perhaps Nick hadn't made it obvious. He thought he had, but it seemed that men like Hargreaves needed everything to be set out in detail, preferably on pieces of thin paper that they could hold up to the light and inspect. 'Overdraft,' Nick said. 'You know, back me.'

'You mean for manufacture?'

'No. At least, not straight away. It needs proving first.'

'And how do you propose to do that?'

Nick took a deep breath. 'By riding it at Silverstone. The British Grand Prix.'

He might as well have said the Epsom Derby for all the reaction he got. Hargreaves stirred a couple of the sheets of paper around on the desk, as if looking for reassurance that his familiar world was in there somewhere amongst its mass of pedantic detail. 'I see,' he said.

'It's a unique piece of engineering. If I can prove it on the track . . . well, the sky's the limit.'

'And that's where a manufacturer would come in?'

'Right.'

'So why don't you go to one?'

'They'd take it over and that's not what I want.'

'But if it's as good as you say,' Hargreaves persisted, 'they'd pay a fortune, surely.'

'I want to *ride* it. Look, if I do well, the whole world will see this new kind of bike, different from anything they've ever seen before . . .' Nick trailed off. Hargreaves was obviously unreachable – at least, to a dreamer in an ill-fitting suit with the distinct signs of a fading black eye and a split lip. He was shuffling the papers together and pushing them across the desk towards Nick. It seemed his ten minutes were up. And up yours, Mister Hargreaves.

The door leading out of the Assistant Manager's office was half wood panelling and half glass, enough to screen out the timid bustle of the rest of the bank. There was a nervous young man waiting outside with a roll of drawings under his arm; best suit hardly ever worn, hair rumpled, glazed look in the eyes – Nick recognized a fellow-failure when he saw one, except that this supplicant didn't look as if he'd spent the weekend on the wrong end of an Aunt Sally stall; and when the Assistant Manager's secretary smiled at him in a way she hadn't smiled at Nick and said, 'Looks like he's free. I think you can go in now,' the young man's chances seemed to be elevated considerably.

'I hope you haven't invented Concorde or something,' Nick said as they passed between two desks. 'He'll ask you how many feathers it's got.'

It was after ten when he got to the garage, nearly half-past when he reached the stores. Wiggins came tumbling out of his office before Nick had got his hand on the door.

'Nick!' he called. 'Nick, I want a word with you.'

Nick waited, strangely out of place in his suit amidst the oil and the noise. Jack Davis was still nursing his new radio – he snatched it to his chest every time Cider walked by – and it was adding its brash rhythm to the bang and clatter of the workshops. Nick raised both his hands in a weary gesture of surrender.

'Okay, Wiggy,' he said. 'You don't have to tell me. You're right, I'm late, I should have told you and I'm not worth the money they pay me. Couldn't interest you in a Yamaha seven-fifty, could I? New slicks, ready to race?'

'There's been an official complaint,' Wiggins said, half pleading with him to take it seriously.

'Oh,' Nick said, and looked around for a suitably-afflicted expression from Davis. He could just be seen between a couple of cars, pretending not to listen but obviously straining to take it all in. 'It could be infectious. Does Cider know about this?'

'It's serious, Nick. Everybody's had to get their own spares – it's chaos in there.'

So they went through the door as Davis stopped pretending and emerged from his bay, wiping his hands on an oily rag. For once his normal scowl was replaced by a grin; on him, it still looked ugly.

If not absolute chaos, the stores were certainly in confusion; nobody could understand the microfiche stock record system, and each mechanic had been rummaging around for the spares he needed; opening boxes at random, sticking them back onto the shelves wherever there was a gap and climbing over each other in their search. Brenda, the girl on the customer desk, was busily fending off a constant stream of telephone enquiries. As Wiggins and Nick stood in the doorway one of the mechanics pushed past with an armload of boxes, spilling a couple of stainless steel clips onto the floor as he went.

'Proper old fuck-up you've made here, sunshine,' he said cheerfully.

'See?' said Wiggins, almost apologetically. 'One more day like this, and you're fired. That's the management's position and it's official. There's nothing I can do.'

'Don't worry, Wiggy,' Nick said. 'There's not going to be another day like this.'

'Look, Nick, it's not just a case of me letting you get away with it any more. Do you know what I'm saying?'

'Yeah, sure. They're riding you.' He pointed in the vague direction of the front office. 'You shouldn't have let me keep the bike here. Any more and it's your head on the block, and all that.'

'No, it's not that. They don't know about the bike. It's . . . well, it's a lot of other things.'

'Like what?'

'The way you run this place. Wrong orders and things

like that. That's why they're doing it, Nick. That's the real reason.'

'Doing what?'

Wiggins took a deep breath, as if he wanted to get rid of the unpleasantness all in one go. 'Putting you on the pumps and transferring Davis in here. The manager's going to tell everybody at four o'clock.'

Wiggins was surprised to find that Nick was less than devastated by the news; certainly he found the idea outrageous, but mostly because it seemed to amuse him. 'On the pumps?' he said. 'Out there, filling tanks?'

'I said it's not me.'

'It's not *me*, either.'

'I'm sorry, Nick,' Wiggins said quietly. 'Really, I am.'

Nick looked around the stores as if he were seeing the place for the last time. 'Will you do something for me, Wiggy?' he said pleasantly. 'Will you tell 'em to stuff it?'

Wiggins smiled, unable to resist the idea for a moment, but when he snapped back to reality Nick was disappearing through the door at the back of the stores to the small stockroom where the Yamaha was kept. 'Hey, Nick,' Wiggins said, starting to follow, 'don't do anything stupid, now. Nick?'

Every head in the stores turned at the almighty roar that suddenly burst from the stockroom. The Yamaha had fired first time and Nick was pouring in the power to keep the engine turning over, as he came nosing out through the doorway and guided the leading wheel into the nearest alley between two shelves. People had to skip out of the way as he let in the clutch and ploughed through a couple of boxes and loose packing; somebody was shouting, no more than a thin and indistinct rattle under the Yamaha's war cry as Nick increased his speed down the shelves and hit the thin ply door which led through to the workshop, splintering it and slamming it back, as the motor-noise and the burning-oil stink erupted into the larger open area.

First he hit a toolbox, but he carried straight on, watching for treacherous oil patches on the floor as he bumped over a couple of air lines and sent the pressure hammers attached to them lashing around like angry snakes. Jack Davis's bay was ahead and to the left; he knocked a rusty silencer that had been left lying, smashing it into oxide-dust and sending it spinning into an empty drum. As the drum bounced aside and Davis scuttled to safety between the cars, Nick saw the item that he was aiming for and revved as he threw the bike into line. There was a satisfying sound of delicate parts shattered, first under the front wheel and then under the back, then Nick was scattering onlookers again as he charged for the big double doors and the outside, sliding out into the car park without stopping and gunning through to the road.

The garage was strangely silent as the engine noise was carried away into the distance, echoing for a while in the wind across the rooftops before fading altogether. Only Cider Jones seemed unworried by the display, sauntering across the track-wreathed concrete to Davis's bay.

Jack Davis emerged from his hiding place. His toolbox had been upset and the spanners and wrenches thrown across the floor; his lunchbox had burst open so that his sandwiches were no more than an ugly smear on the oil. He bent and started numbly to collect the wrenches together as Cider came level and stopped.

'Hey, Davis?' he said, bending down. Davis looked up and saw that Cider was lifting the shattered case of his new radio. 'Why don't you watch TV, man, like everybody else?'

It was too much. Davis grunted and threw the wrench at Cider. It was a hefty piece of iron, turning lazily as it came in for a bone-splitting impact, but Cider simply reached up at the last possible moment and picked it out of the air.

Everybody was quiet. Davis felt the blood draining from his face as he realized what he'd started. Cider was holding the wrench easily in one hand and the shattered radio in the other, and the pleasant gloss of wit and ease had gone from his eyes, leaving them flashing with danger; but then the warning faded and Cider shrugged. 'Tough job,' he said, applying the ridiculously large spanner to the radio's mangled innards, 'but I'll do what I can.'

FOURTEEN

Nick cleaned the Yamaha up before he sold it, and replaced some of the more flagrant cannibalizations with parts from his well-worn stock. Julie came around to the flat and they had a few cans of beer to say goodbye to an old friend, and then she went off to spend the afternoon shopping for dinner, whilst he ran the bike down to the showroom in the back of the van. He knew that the owner wanted the bike for display rather than re-sale, so what the hell, Nick thought as he looked on some of his rather dodgy repairs, as long as he doesn't actually try to *start* it while I'm still in the shop.

When the actual transaction was made Nick got the impression that the owner was mainly delighted by the bike's rough and track-worn appearance; but he didn't stay around to observe whether that delight lasted as the exhaust system fell off in the middle of the showroom.

When he arrived back at the flat, dinner was cooking and there was a pile of groceries on the table, more than they really needed.

'What's all this?' he said, and Julie put her head around the partition that divided the kitchen from the sitting room.

'Dinner for tonight, then breakfast,' she said.

'Breakfast?'

'You don't intend sending me home without any, do you?'

He grinned, and went through to join her. 'Who said I was sending you home at all?'

*

In the days that followed, Nick found that there were many ways of expressing indifference and disinterest, and he was on the receiving end of them all. Julie started the ball rolling with a visit to the commercial section of the local library, making lists of firms from trade directories and industry publications. They noted anything that seemed likely to throw up a possible backer, from big corporations in the city to small engineering firms in the suburbs.

Big banks were hopeless, Nick realized in the middle of his second interview. All assistant managers seemed to be clones of Hargreaves, and they rehearsed the same sequence of pained expressions as he tried to explain about the Silver Dream. Nick didn't even wait for the inevitable brush-off, but bundled his papers together in mid-sentence and walked out, leaving the Hargreaves-clone with his jaw hanging open. Outside on the pavement he gave Julie a progress report under the disapproving eye of the doorman, and then they went on to the next appointment.

'Cross all the bloody banks off the list,' he said as they set off.

Julie tried the next one, a factory that made engine parts and industrial castings. Nick had specifically okayed it because there was no involvement with bikes or racing, so there was little chance that they would attempt to grab all of the Silver Dream for themselves. His estimation was too accurate; they didn't want *any* of it.

'No big factories,' he told Julie, and the list shrank a little more.

Next was a small foundry on the fringe of the inner city, an old-fashioned and noisy brick building, lined inside with cast-iron stairways and catwalks. They had to find their own way to a tiny office overlooking a vast open space where molten metal flowed and hammers rang below. They'd had polite indifference, brusque indifference; now they got rude indifference from a fat bearded man in shirtsleeves; on the way out Nick made as if to throw himself over the safety rail of the catwalk.

'I know,' Julie said, pulling him back. 'No *small* factories.'

Then came the city corporations: luxurious suites of offices hidden like tiny warrens in immense monolithic structures in the Barbican, towering edifices of glass and concrete with all the personality of an unlettered gravestone. Here they at least got a polite hearing from junior executives who nodded interestedly, and were served coffee by secretaries with hideous nail varnish and an excess of expensive makeup. But the results were little different; a promise to pass the proposal on for further consideration and an assurance that they would be contacted; and that, they somehow knew as they travelled back to earth, was the end of it.

They went from tower to tower, from Rothwell Consolidated to Holbein International, and when Nick came out, dizzy and airsick, Julie took his elbow and guided him along to the Heracles Corporation, passing through the foyer and under the security cameras to yet another elevator.

Nick sighed depressively as they rode up to the seventh floor. 'Why don't we just . . .' he began.

'You can't,' Julie cut in. 'If you cross off the big corporations, you'll have no more list.'

Like all the other offices, this suite had carpet as thick and deep as uncut grass and a reception area with low chairs in reasonable imitation of leather. It was an area that seemed to be somehow cut off from space and time, as well as from the city far below whose smells and noises could never penetrate.

Benson came out to talk to them amongst the old magazines and the potted plants, and he offered them the inevitable coffee. By this stage Nick felt like asking for a bucket to be sick in afterwards, but he gave a fixed and glassy smile and nodded.

Benson was young, hardly more than thirty, but had the good clothes and the authoritative manner which marked him as somebody who had risen fast in the organization and would probably continue rising. He seemed interested, but then so had all the others – it was probably an illusive skill that all executives acquired. Behind the polish, his heavy-lidded eyes gave nothing away.

'Mister Freeman,' he said after Nick had gone through his explanation of the origin and capabilities of the Silver Dream, 'I'll come right to the point. It saves a lot of misunderstanding, and I believe in giving quick decisions.' He turned one of the plans to look at it again; it was becoming distinctly curly from being handled. 'Financial dealings depend a lot on collateral. It's a matter of who pays if the scheme fails. Companies can put up their factories as collateral. Individuals can put up their houses.'

'Mister Benson,' Julie said, seeing the familiar spectre of disappointment approaching. 'He told you, he doesn't have a house.'

'No. He's got something much better.'

'A rented room,' Nick said gloomily.

'The motorbike. I'll need to see it, of course, and get an expert opinion – but if it's as good as it looks on paper, I'm prepared to put up four thousand.'

For a moment they'd heard only what they expected to hear, and Nick almost reached out resignedly to gather in the Silver Dream documents yet again. But he stopped himself in time and stared at Benson, who was outlining the simple terms of the loan. 'In a year from now,' he went on, 'either you pay me back *five* thousand, or I take the bike. Full manufacturing rights, patents, the lot. What do you say? Do I take it we've got a deal?'

The terms were murderous by any conventional calculation of interest, but then it was a considerable gamble, and even at twenty-five per cent, it was an encouraging display of confidence on Benson's part. He led them through into the inner office to draw up a contract, snapping on the lights to counter the fading glow of the sunset outside. As Nick and Julie looked around they could see that the walls of the office were a dense mass of neatly framed pictures, each lit by its own spotlight. There were racing bikes, vintage motorcycles, speedway shots, trials bikes, drag bikes, custom bikes; Benson observed their surprise and said, 'Lovely, aren't they? One day I'll show you the real thing.'

'Real thing?' Julie said.

'Well, yes,' said Benson, looking for the first time a little blank. 'I'm a collector. That's why you came here, isn't it?'

Nick and Julie looked at each other, and an unspoken warmth passed between them. Someone, somewhere, seemed to be giving Nick Freeman the break he so desperately needed. He turned to Benson and said, 'Would you like to see *my* bike now? It's outside in the van.'

The lidded, emotion-masking expression seemed to fall from Benson at the offer, and undiluted boyish interest shouldered the tough businessman aside. 'Really?' he said with undisguised enthusiasm.

Later that night, after all the excitement and the celebration that they could devise between them, they lay exhausted and relaxed on the bed with only a single sheet between them and the warm summer night.

'Do you believe it?' Nick said, gazing up at the coloured patterns on the ceiling from the street outside. 'I mean, really believe it?'

'Absolutely,' said Julie.

'Neither do I.' He reached over to the bedside table and picked up the cheque, lifting it to where it could catch the light from the window and become legible. He'd never seen so much money in one place before; not his own, with his name on the cheque. He held it out so Julie could see it. 'What time do the banks open?' he said, and she started to laugh.

The next day Julie went out for more shopping; not food this time, but parts, tools and accessories which Nick had listed for her in precise detail, including order numbers whenever he knew them. As soon as she had gone he started to put the flat in order, moving the furniture back to the walls and spreading out old dust sheets and newspaper to protect the carpet. Then he watched out of the window until he saw Mrs Buonaguidi making her eleven o'clock visit to the market, making sure that she went all the way down the street and around the corner without turning back for some forgotten item. Then he ran down and cleared the hall of obstacles, pinned the door back with a wedge of folded newspaper, and manhandled the Silver Dream from the back of the van into the hall and up the stairs. When it was safely in the room he went back for the supporting stands and tools; some were his own, some had been 'liberated' from the garage, most of them were Greg's. He set up a small collapsible lathe, filled the electricity meter, and began to strip the bike down.

Julie arrived back at about four o'clock and found Nick in blue overalls and safety goggles. He was carefully shaving metal from the circumference of a gear-wheel the size of his fist, and such was his concentration that he didn't look up straight away when she came in. She crossed to the table and dumped her cartons, boxes and packages on it, and then turned to look around the room. The Silver Dream was upright in its clamps in the middle of the floor, only half-assembled; its component parts were scattered all around the room, laid out on the floor, the chairs, the windowsill.

'Hey,' she said as the high-pitched noise of the grindstone stopped, 'what's happening here?'

'Don't step on anything,' Nick said without looking up. He bent to scribble something on a note-pad on the floor.

'What's going on?'

'I'm making it six ounces lighter.'

'Ah.' She nodded sagely. 'You sure you know what you're doing?'

He slowly raised his eyes to her, and shook his head with exasperation. 'I once took my grandfather's watch to pieces.'

'Oh, fine. You'll be okay, then.'

'Couldn't get it back together again, though,' he added, and turned back to look closely at the gear-wheel.

She came forward and put her arms around his neck. 'But you're older now.'

'Not a lot.'

Julie smiled, and kissed the top of his head, and then disentangled herself and walked back over to the table. 'Listen,' she said, 'I picked up the carburettors and the brake pipes and the pads, but then I ran out of cash and they wouldn't take a cheque.'

'Why not?' Nick said, dusting his hands off on his overalls and wandering over to take a look.

She seemed troubled. 'Don't know me, I guess. But then at Barton Motors . . . maybe you should sit down for this.'

'Don't tell me they can't do it?' he said sharply.

'They can do it, no problem. Trouble is, they won't.'

'What do you mean, won't? Greg spent thousands with Bartons. They've still got the dies, the casts, everything!' He looked around for the phone, forgetting for the moment where he'd moved it. 'What the hell do they think they're playing at?'

'Hold it, Nick. Before you call them, you ought to know something.'

'What?'

'Your brother owed them money.'

'So we'll pay it. How much?'

'Three thousand.'

Nick paused with the phone halfway to his ear, and then put it slowly down. 'Can't be,' he said, his confusion showing. 'Greg always paid – everything . . .'

'They showed me the bills. It's thirty-one hundred, and that's without interest of three percent a month on account of late payment.'

Nick didn't comment straight away. He gazed down at the dismantled bike with a look that said haunted, trapped.

'I got some food,' Julie offered. 'Do you want to eat?'

He didn't seem to hear. 'Why? I mean, why didn't they say this before?'

'Bartons thought your sister-in-law still owned the bike. They were holding the bills back.'

'Yeah. Know what my dad used to say? As one door closes, another one slams in your face.'

She moved over and put her arms around him again. He didn't respond. 'I know, honey,' she said. 'But . . . well, it's not the end of the world'

'No?' Nick said bitterly. 'Take three thousand from the four thousand Benson lent me. I need disc valves, standby frame . . . it's bloody impossible.' He kicked out and sent some inoffensive minor component skittering across the floor.

Julie tried to be soothing. 'There's always some way out. Let me call Benson.'

'*Benson*? You didn't read the contract? I *guaranteed* there were no legal or money problems. I signed a document saying the bike was free of debt, I was free of debt, the whole fucking *world* was free of debt! That's about the only thing he insisted on. No need for a physical, enter any race I like – but is the goddam bike really mine and *is it free of debt*?'

He dropped into the chair. She went and knelt by him, concerned and a little apprehensive. 'Nick?' she said, stroking his hand. 'Nick, listen to me. Sometimes I think I'm crazy. And maybe you're a little crazy too. I mean, what are we trying to prove? You lost your job—'

'I walked out,' he corrected as a matter of pride.

'That was my fault. Now you're in debt, and I guess that's my fault too. I started this, and . . . well, I don't even know why any more.'

Nick was barely listening. 'Just to show 'em,' he said, more to himself than anything else. 'Just once.'

'You're not listening. I'm trying to tell you I was wrong. I was trying to get back at somebody. Trying to find . . . maybe a gladiator, I don't know. I just wanted to hit out – can you understand that? But it doesn't matter any more.'

Nick slowly turned his head to stare at her. 'It does to me,' he said.

'Don't let it,' she urged. 'I came here to start school again, and Bruce just happened to be here . . .'

'Bruce?' Nick said, uncomprehending. 'Who gives a shit about Bruce?'

'Well,' she tried to explain, 'if it's not important—'

'Not important? It's everything. Ever since I can remember. Probably the greatest race in the world.'

For a moment, Julie was utterly disoriented. She'd been so self-centred in her battle with Bruce McBride that she'd never even considered that Nick might be motivated by something other than a desire to please her. Maybe she'd started him off, given the emotional push to his ambitions that he needed, but now he was moving she realized that there was no way she could simply turn him off again.

'Oh, Nick,' she said, almost unable to speak with the choking weight of her self-deception. 'I'm sorry . . . what can I do?'

'Tell people how I almost raced at Silverstone. Tell them while I'm filling their tanks.'

Slowly, she stood up and moved to the door. She collected her purse almost absently on the way. She stopped in the doorway and looked back. 'I'm sorry,' she said, aware of the pitiful inadequacy of the words.

Nick nodded. Julie left, closing the door carefully behind her. He was still for almost a minute, staring at the floor. Then he abruptly grabbed the gear-wheel and flung it, smashing through the partition into the kitchen and raining broken glass down onto the work surfaces, as it bounced back from an ugly dent in the plaster of the far wall.

FIFTEEN

Julie telephoned the garage next day and eventually managed to get hold of Cider. It was impossible to hold a conversation because of the background noise on the workshop phone, but Cider said that he could get away early, no problem, and so they agreed to meet in the afternoon.

She was waiting at a window table in the cafe when the old Ford van, with its innumerable stickers and racing logos, drew up outside. Cider hopped out and slid the door closed behind him, looking more as if he'd just stepped off the dancefloor than out of a hot and oily workplace.

He came straight over and greeted her like an old friend, in spite of the fact that it was less than a couple of weeks since they'd met for the first time. He seemed to approve of the cafe with its bare brick and crisp linen, a little corner of taste and quiet in an otherwise insensitive world.

She told him about Nick, and her horrendously ill-judged attempt to use him to get revenge on Bruce McBride, and of the financial difficulties related to the Silver Dream. Then she told him what she proposed doing about it, and asked him if he thought she would be right.

Cider thought it over for a moment. 'He's a maniac,' he said. 'You know that? He's crazy.'

'That's not what I asked you.'

'All right. He's the best rider I've ever seen.'

'Cider,' she said, trying to pin him down to be serious, 'it's important.'

Cider pushed his coffee cup aside and took a deep breath. 'Nick . . . well, he's like a brother to me, okay? We did the club races and the small circuits, and we had some good times. But *Silverstone*? Baby, that's something else.'

'Listen,' she said, 'I know you think I'm as crazy as he is. But if I went through with this, would you help?'

'Ah, Julie . . .' he said, shaking his head as if the words simply didn't exist that he could use to get through to her.

'You keep avoiding my question.'

'Mind if I ask *you* something? You haven't . . . I mean you're not getting too involved with Nick, are you?'

'It sure didn't start out that way.'

'But it is now, right?'

'I don't know,' she said evasively. 'Maybe. Look, all I'm asking, Cider, is . . . if I did it, would you stand behind him?'

'Suppose they won't give me the time off?'

'Would you at least ask? Cider, it's the only thing he ever wanted in his whole life.'

'Crazy,' Cider said, but he seemed to be turning the idea over in his mind.

'Please, Cider.'

He looked around the adjacent tables and gave a long sigh, as if he were waving an irrevocable goodbye to some part of his life. Then he turned back to Julie and lit up his most dazzling smile.

'Only because you're so pretty,' he told her.

She leaned across the table and hugged him hard, scattering the napkins and the salt cellar. 'Now we're all crazy,' she said. 'Right?'

'Yeah,' he beamed, 'but some of us are elegant, witty, charming and handsome too, remember.'

It was late when Nick reached Bond Street Underground, and the folding metal gates had long been drawn across the entrances and locked. But this was where the transport office had told him to be, and when he listened hard he could hear the distant sounds of subterranean activity, so he took hold of the gates and rattled them. The sound echoed off around the darkened station and for a while there was no response, so he rattled again.

After a few minutes there was the faint knock of hard boots on concrete somewhere below. A man came into sight on the far side of the gates; he was wearing overalls and a safety helmet and he carried a large heavy-duty flashlight. He stopped well back and looked at Nick warily.

'What do you want?' he said.

'I'm Nick Freeman,' he told the man. 'I've come to see my dad.'

The man unlocked the gates and let him through, and then led him into the deserted station. The ticket barriers were open and the escalators were still, and lighting had been cut to a dim emergency minimum as they descended to the Central line.

Nick waited alone on the empty platform. Across the rails on the curving tunnel wall, a couple of new posters glistened with fresh paste. Far away down the black hole at the end of the track occasional blue flashes indicated the approach of a maintenance wagon.

The wagon rolled out into the light of the station and braked to a halt, and the repairmen on board clambered down to check on the Bond Street signalling system. Nick thrust his hands deep into his pockets and walked over. He stopped by one of the men working on the track.

Jack Freeman looked up in surprise. 'Nick,' he said, 'what are you doing here?'

'Thought I'd say hello. Have you got a second?'

Freeman was a broad, tough-looking man, and he'd carried some of his strength and agility into middle age. He stepped over the live rail and the tracks and scrambled up onto the platform. Then he looked back with a little apprehension at the rest of the crew, and called out, 'Ben! Check four and seven for me, will you? I won't be a minute.'

Ben Ransome looked up briefly from the far side of the track and signalled his assent. Nick sensed his father's worry and said, 'I won't keep you. I know you're busy.'

'What is it, son?' Jack Freeman said, frowning. He sensed that a problem lay behind the visit.

'Thought I'd drop by . . . you know.'

'Last time you came down here was when you were a kid. Now what's wrong?'

They started to walk slowly along the platform, away from the crew. Freeman seemed to be pleased to see Nick, but wasn't sure how to show it. 'Money, mainly,' Nick admitted.

'How much do you need?'

'I wouldn't ask you for money, dad. You know that.'

'So what is it?'

'Tina gave me Greg's bike. Did she tell you?'

'What, his big one?'

'That's it, the Silver Dream.'

'And it's not paid for,' Freeman said, striking immediately to the heart of the trouble. 'Is that it?'

True as it was, it wasn't the reason for Nick's presence, and he hurried to make it clear. 'No. Well, yes, but that's *my* problem. What I wanted to ask you is a sort of personal thing. I've been walking around half the night thinking about it. Now I'm here, I don't know how to start.'

'Listen, Nicky, I've known you since the day you were born, so don't piss me around. Whatever it is, just say it, all right?'

'Okay. What made you give up boxing?'

Freeman stopped walking, and Nick turned to him. There was puzzlement on the older man's face. 'Is that what you came to ask? I got too old.'

'You've always said that, haven't you? I worked it out once. You were only twenty-six when you quit the ring, Dad.'

Jack Freeman sighed and looked down at his boots. They were dusty and scuffed by years of clambering over obstacles and wading through tunnel-filth in the dark. 'I don't know what brought this on, Nick. But when you've got a family, you don't mess with dangerous sports. Some do, but not me.'

'If it hadn't been for us, would you have gone on?'

Freeman's attention was taken by the track gang for a moment– or was he covering something? 'Ben!' he shouted. 'Why's that red light out?' he turned back to Nick. 'Look,' he said, 'I've got to go.'

'Would you?'

'I might have. Why?' And then something seemed to fall into place. 'I get it,' he went on, 'Carol's pregnant and she wants you to give up the race game, is that it?' He smiled ruefully. 'Comes to us all in the end, you know.'

Nick didn't want to get side-tracked into explanations about Carol, not when he was so close to finding out the answer to his question – an answer that he suspected he knew already. 'But you would have gone on,' he pressed, 'wouldn't you?'

Freeman looked at his son with a firm and steady gaze. 'I'd have been the bloody Champion if I'd gone on, and that's the truth.'

All of a sudden Nick's world seemed a little firmer, his ambitions less hopeless. 'Yeah. Dad, I'm going to embarrass you. I love you. Goodnight.' And then, before the scene got sticky and impossible for them to handle, he went.

He walked around a little longer, but the worst was over

and his faith in himself came slowly creeping back. The first cold greyness of dawn was on the streets as he arrived home, kicking through the litter spread by exploring tramps during the night.

In the sitting-room, he stopped and looked around. There was enough light to see by, but he switched on a table lamp to make sure he wasn't deceived. All around the room were neat rows of packages, wrapped and ribboned like birthday presents and laid out in a numbered order which seemed to correspond to the blueprint plan that was pinned out on the table. The Silver Dream was in the middle as he'd left it, and there was a green package on the handlebars; except that it *wasn't* a package, he saw as he moved closer and reached out, it was a thick, wad of new bills, too many even to estimate as he riffled through them.

The bedroom door was slightly open, the room shadowy behind closed curtains. As he turned on the light a shape stirred in the bed. He crossed over and gently pulled the covers from Julie's face. She looked up at him, blinking in the light, her hair tousled from sleeping. He held up the money.

'What's this?' he said quietly.

She tried to make light of it. 'That? It's kind of . . . like a ticket to ride.'

He sat slowly on the bed and gently took her face in his hands. He kissed her and sat back. 'Would you mind telling me what's going on?'

'*You're* going on. And if you don't get in training soon—' she poked him in the midriff '—you're not going to make it. I checked and you have exactly three weeks.'

'No, wait a minute. Where'd this money come from?'

'The car. I sold my MG, okay?'

SIXTEEN

Three weeks to get race-fit; a tough schedule, and one that couldn't easily be followed in the city. There was the additional problem of getting the bike together over the same time, and since he was limited to using the noisier pieces of equipment when Mrs Buonaguidi was out of the house – no more than a couple of hours each day, at the most – and turning the motor over was out of the question. It was Julie's idea that they should get out into the country, where he could work on the bike without distraction and get tightened up with exercise in between times. When Nick asked her what kind of exercise she had in mind she tapped him on the nose warningly and gave him a series of development charts she'd worked out.

'I'll die!' he gasped as he read them.

'I know what I'm doing. Everything's graduated to get you to a peak for the race without exhausting you. I've made out some diet sheets, as well.'

He looked over the second sheaf of papers that she handed him, the grapefruit and the yoghurt and the bananas and the bran, and here and there, peeping coyly out like some decadent treat, a little boiled fish. 'What the hell's Liquid Liver?' he said.

'Strength in a bottle. You won't need a lathe, you'll be able to hammer out parts with your bare hands.'

'Are you sure I'll survive all this?'

'It worked for Jimmy.'

A hotel was out of the question. They had a little money to spare, but not so much they could throw it away, and whilst the Ford van could just about take the bike along with all the gear they needed, there wasn't enough space to sleep as well. So in the end they compromised and hired a bigger van, a capacious red monster that was more a truck with room enough for the bags and the supplies and the sleeping bags, still leaving enough space to scratch. They loaded up early in the morning and were heading for the West Country before the city had started to come to life.

They found an old airfield on the map, a vast deserted plot with crumbling hangars and huge, rotting buildings. Much of the concrete was broken and cracked by thrusting weeds, but the main runway was in reasonable shape for testing the bike, as long as he didn't wander too far from the centre-line.

The old control tower had no glass in its windows, and the plaster from the ceiling had made the short and direct trip down to the floor. But the warm July winds had dried the open building out, and by the end of the afternoon they'd got it sufficiently cleared to set up a tidy camp. The evening meal was the first of the new regime: cottage cheese and salad washed down with juice to flush the lingering poisons of junk food out of his system, and so many vitamins he thought he'd rattle.

The next morning she woke him early and sent him out to run around the perimeter of the field before a high-roughage breakfast. He thought it would kill him, and he arrived back panting and sick. After half an hour he felt better, though, and took a certain pride in having made it all the way around without actually slowing to a walk, so she sent him out again. He spent the afternoon working on the bike, and in the evening he tried a few simple isometrics before he was allowed to knock off and relax.

That first day set the pattern for those that were to follow. They went to sleep in the back of the van shortly after dark and awoke around dawn, and Nick found on his early run that his style improved and his time reduced as his pace came back. He actually began to enjoy the health foods that Julie had waiting for him. Each day he was weighed on a pair of bathroom scales and his main measurements taken and plotted onto a chart, and it was satisfying to see a graphic demonstration of his growing fitness.

If the mornings were for his body, the afternoons were for the Silver Dream. Every part and every back-up spare were tested on the bike, and when he was confident with his familiarity, he measured out a mile along the best-preserved sections of runway and perimeter road and began to run the bike at speed, developing his own skills to suit its unique handling characteristics. It was far lighter and more responsive than any other bike he'd ridden and the temptation was to over-correct after each manoeuvre. But as he became confident of the feel of the machine, he began to shave complete seconds off his time for the mile, as Julie measured it on her stopwatch.

In the evenings he was allowed an occasional low-carbohydrate lager. Julie noted exactly how much he drank and then adjusted his diet over the next couple of days to compensate, reducing his carefully-weighed portions accordingly. They'd listen to the radio or study detailed plans of the Silverstone circuit; off the grid and into the sharp bend of Copse Corner, down through the kink of Maggotts Curve to the forty-five degree bend of Becketts Corner and then out into Hangar straight for a heads-down race to the South Grandstands at Stowe Corner. Heading North as the crowds began to grow noticeably denser again, Abbey Curve and Woodcote Corner and then through the pits and the grandstands to lean hard into Copse Corner again and another lap. Nick built the picture in his mind, selecting his gear changes and picking the best places to break away and make a bid to overtake, working out where it was best to be defensive and force those behind to hold back – and, of course, where the same was likely to be done to him.

He ate Muesli until he felt he was turning into a raisin; he called it mouse-dirt and chewed each mouthful for what seemed like an age, but he had to admit that he'd never felt better. The bike ran like the dream that it was named, and he made careful note of every minor calibration that seemed to increase its performance. When he rode in the afternoon sun the Silver Dream flashed and glittered and seemed almost to fly; Nick seemed to lose contact with time and reality. Speed on the Silver Dream was not deadly, it was simply appropriate, the only fit medium for it to come entirely into its own. Nick didn't feel that he was cheating death – he was outstripping it and leaving it far behind. He and the Silver Dream were unstoppable.

Nights they spent in the back of the van, the three of them together: Nick, Julie and Greg's legacy, its powerful shape in tense repose in the dark beside them.

Julie awoke and frowned. She thought she'd heard something, but she wasn't sure. It had never bothered Nick, but at nights she felt a little vulnerable so far from help but so easy to reach; the only time they'd actually seen anybody over the last couple of weeks had been when they'd driven into the village to pick up some shopping.

Nick was still asleep. He'd obviously heard nothing. But he came wide awake in an instant when somebody banged on the side of the van. They both grabbed for the flashlight together and managed only to knock it way out of reach. Nick groped for it without success as whoever was outside moved around to the tail shutter of the van and began to explore the catch.

'Sod it,' Nick gasped. 'Where the hell are my bloody jeans?'

He was halfway out of the sleeping bag when the shutter

was lifted a couple of feet, the vibration shaking the whole van. A powerful flashlight burst in and blinded them; Nick was hopelessly tangled, and he started kicking hard to get the bag off his legs. The flashlight turned away from them.

'Anybody here use a little wit and elegance?' Cider said casually as he turned the beam onto himself.

Julie found the van's interior light and snapped it on. 'You bastard!' Nick said incredulously. 'That could have been *anyone*!' But he couldn't keep up the indignation, pleased as he was to see Cider. Julie bounced over to the tailgate to give him a hug.

'Most honoured,' Cider said. 'But, lovely as you are, *there's* the lady I really came to see.'

They looked around. The Silver Dream gleamed modestly.

SEVENTEEN

The official timetable of events for the British Grand Prix at Silverstone spread over three days, but activity started some time before that. At the beginning of the week the paddock area, a fenced-off reservation of tarmac and grass behind the pits, was almost deserted. The lawns were uneven and bad, rutted into rough tracks by seasons of shortcuts and misuse, and in the open windy spaces the litter of old meetings danced and played.

The track was more or less in order when the first caravans and transporters began to arrive. The grid positions had been painted fresh and the crash barriers had been set on the curves, baled hay and springy wire several layers deep and anchored by breakaway posts. The massive hoardings with the bright sponsors' messages had been erected where the TV emplacements would get the best and least obstructive view of them.

First came the advance guard of the big boys, the really immense works-sponsored outfits who had haggled for the best pitches near to the track. Truckloads of tenting and scaffolding were unloaded and assembled to become luxury canvas lounges, much grander advertisements than the spartan guest pits which overlooked the track by the paddock. As the space-age pieces of tent design were hoisted and fastened the smaller operations with their tents and trailers came bumping over the metal bridge to the inside of the track enclosure to fill up the gaps, until by Friday and the first day of official practice the paddock was like one large, sprawling camp-site. The low huts that seemed to be the paddock's only fixed structures beyond the brick and concrete of the pits were unboarded and tenanted to sell burgers, doughnuts, warm, canned drinks, and disposable plastic cups of beer.

Around the outside of the track the first of the hard-line fans began to collect, pitching their tents and their caravans right up against the grassy bank that was raised to a height of about fifteen feet between the grandstands. The really enterprising ones brought scaffolding and erected their own small stands on top of the bank, claiming their places for the weekend ahead.

Nick rolled into the paddock on the Thursday, and was allocated a fairly decent pitch behind the pits. The hired van got him a few laughs – hey, man, who's this Avis Racing? – but no vehicle, however sober or extravagant, could seem out of place here. There were big American tourers, custom jobs, small and ropey rattletraps; all were painted and lettered with the names of riders, owners and sponsors.

Each pitch had a roped-off area to hold back crowding and to give room for the bikes to be put on modest display. When teams weren't working with their own machines the main occupation was to wander around the paddock with a studiously casual air weighing up the opposition. There was noise, and the smell of oil mixed with frying bacon most of the day. There was excitement which was slowly winding like a mainspring.

The Silver Dream brought a lot of attention and a few enquiries, but Nick gave nothing away. He sat at the breakfast table and chomped at his Muesli, nodding and smiling at each expression of interest. 'New design,' was the most he would offer, and racing protocol prevented anybody from pressing him further.

A couple of tiny puttering paddock bikes, no more than 80cc child scramblers, dodged and wove through the people on the narrow access road as Cider ambled easily over to Nick's enclosure. Most of the teams seemed to delight in using the tiniest runabouts they could find, and most of the day the site rang as with the buzzing of hornets as the bikes commuted from trailers to pits.

Julie smiled a greeting and Cider came over to the folding metal table. He was about to speak when he saw what Nick was eating, and he plucked the plate from under Nick's nose to stare into it in disbelief.

'She's got you eating *mouse* dirt?' he said incredulously. He was wearing his garage dungarees and his 'lucky' hat, a shapeless woollen pull-on.

'Don't ask,' Nick said. The wafting smells of frying sausages and bacon from the Calor stoves all around were giving him poignant feelings of nostalgia.

Julie consulted the list in front of her for Cider's benefit. 'It has two milligrams of vitamins B1, B2, B6 and B12; fifty milligrams of ascorbic acid and four hundred units of vitamin D in every ounce. The honey's for energy.'

'All those vitamins, why ain't you Superman?'

'I told you,' Nick said, reaching for the bowl. 'Don't ask.'

Cider unshouldered the tyre he'd been carrying and sat down on one of the folding tubular steel beach chairs. 'Listen,' he said, 'when you've finished that great repast I want you to take a look at the spare con-rods. They're the wrong size.'

'I know,' Nick said, 'they cocked the order up. I've got another consignment in the van somewhere.'

'Okay,' Cider said, and he sauntered over to the van. The tail-shutter was open a few inches, and he hooked a hand underneath and lifted it easily. After a minute he was back with the new con-rods.

'Hey,' he said, 'I took a walk over the other side of the track just now. There's a TV unit setting up, film cameras and everything. They're really getting moving, looks like Sunday's going to be a big day.'

'The Grand Prix always is,' Nick said. 'You get world coverage.'

'That's all very well, but I mean . . . who's going to feed 'em?'

'Don't look at me,' said Julie.

'I said feed 'em, not poison 'em. So what time's he taking the bike out today, boss?'

'He's not. Today's a rest day. Final qualifying laps tomorrow – and after all this he'd better keep up yesterday's times or I'll make sure he eats nothing but mouse dirt and yoghurt for the rest of his life.'

Sunday morning, seven o'clock. It hadn't been light much more than half an hour, and already it was starting. The over-nighters emerged from their tents and caravans, stretching in their rumpled old clothes and shivering a little in the morning chill, swinging their soapbags as they ambled along to the spartan toilet facilities. At the main entrance by Woodcote Corner four lines of cars, vans and bikes were already backing up into the narrow country lanes around the circuit. They were ushered into order by officers of the Northampton and Thames Valley police – smiling now, their smiles perhaps becoming tighter later on. But these were cycle racing crowds, not football yobs, and the problems they offered were simply those which involved the handling of large masses of people. A hundred thousand or more by the afternoon; standing traffic and a two-hour queue to get in by nine. They were trailing in now, but the worst was to come in the evening around six-thirty, when suddenly everybody would be leaving at once.

They bought their tickets from vendors in red nylon coats and shoulder-bags heavy with change, and rolled on a few yards to buy a glossy programme. Then they were at the perimeter road and being waved left onto the one-way circuit, follow the road around and park on the grass outside the bank and the stands. And as the cars and the bikes and the vans and the lorries poured in, sheep nuzzled unconcerned in an adjacent field, heads-down and preoccupied in the grey of the morning.

Already there were limp burgers and warm cokes on sale for iron stomachs. Behind the main Grandstand at the northernmost part of the track, a little commercial sector was developing as licensed traders spread out T shirts, cheap nylon team jackets, hats, brooches, belt buckles, badges. There were stalls, caravan extensions, small marquees and even a converted bus decked out with stickers; here also were the low huts where lines were forming to buy unsold grandstand tickets and paddock transfers which would allow access to the iron footbridge across the track and an excited wander through Team Country. Outside the gathering knot of customers were the green vans of the television outside broadcast link, the end-stop of a fat umbilical of cables which snaked through an under-road culvert to emerge into the Marshals' car park right underneath the main stands.

The best places were already gone. The old hands knew where they were and they claimed them immediately with collapsible frame chairs, garden seats, sheets of polythene spread and anchored by stones. More makeshift stands were erected on the tops of the grassy banks, some of them six or seven feet high and looking decidedly rickety. At nine o'clock the day was really beginning to shape up into an event; muzak started abruptly from the grandstand speakers, and four green single-deck buses filed out onto the track to give free rides around the course, a riders' eye view at a fraction of the speed.

Ten o'clock. The weather still hadn't decided what it was going to do. The forecast was for clear sky and sunshine but there was an obstinate mist hugging the ground. Managers, mechanics and riders stood around looking pensive, wondering whether to fit dry or wet-weather tyres onto their machines. Behind the pits the Marshals were gathering for their instructions, indistinguishable from the crowds other than by their bright sashes.

At around eleven Nick wandered through the lines of cars and caravans to take a look at the placing of the pit that had been allocated to the Silver Dream. No point getting tensed up yet, because the 500cc race wasn't scheduled to start until about three-thirty and there were four events preceding it. People were still pouring over the iron footbridge with their paddock transfer tickets, and it seemed pretty likely that the crowding on this side of the track was going to be a constant feature of the day.

No chance of getting close to the pit right now. The up-and-over door at the trackside end of the workshop was open and a three-deep cluster of interested onlookers were pushing to get sight of a sidecar rig that was to be competing in the first race, a little before twelve. Preceding that would be some showbiz and ballyhoo, a couple of circuits by lorries carrying big-bike displays, guest appearances by a couple of retired riders, names known even in the non-racing world.

Nick crossed the pit apron and pulled himself up to lean on the guardrail that topped the sliproad barrier; across the track the grandstand was more or less full already, scaffolding, bleachers and canvas, topped with flags and crammed with people. In the middle, three storeys above the track was the glass-fronted commentary box and on top of that, distant and forlorn, an unmanned TV camera emplacement. Going to be a big day. You get world coverage.

A large saloon with 'Pace Car' lettered on its side was driving past, as Nick climbed down from the guardrail and walked back towards the paddock. This could be a bad time if he allowed it to be; three weeks of careful buildup of concentration and capability could be wasted by half a day of aimless worrying, rehearsing every move of the competition in his mind so often that his best efforts would have been wasted before he reached the grid.

A bike was firing up, the first to be heard trackside, and there was a distinct wave of excitement all around. The course commentator was telling the crowds about the day ahead and about some of the the personalities who would be racing, heroes whose recent histories and misfortunes were a matter for public concern. Australian Champion Steve Perry on a Suzuki, Giovanni Batista on Kawasaki and Bruce McBride . . . Nick wanted to stop listening, but of course he couldn't simply switch off his hearing. No mention of Nick Freeman; Nick Freeman held no titles, no records, and he wasn't placed anywhere near the top runners when it came to totalling up points for the World Championship– in fact, he wasn't in the running at all. But perhaps, by the end of the afternoon, all that would be changed.

When he'd checked the allocation of the pits earlier, he'd noticed, about three bays down from his own and closer than he would have liked, *res. Trans-World Racing.* Closer than he would have liked, but what the hell. It's what happens out there that counts. Somewhere in the guest pits on the inner curve of Woodcote Corner, Benson was entertaining a couple of Japanese businessmen who had shown an interest in the Silver Dream as a manufacturing possibility; Nick wondered whether he ought to be dutiful and go over to socialize, but he felt that he'd done enough earlier when they'd come around to inspect the bike in the paddock!

He had to relax, become absorbed until the time was

right for concentration and energy. He yawned and moved off towards the van.

After a light lunch – weighed and prescribed by Julie – he lay on top of a bag in the back of the van and tried to sleep. He'd offered Cider a hand with the final adjustments to the machine, but he'd been turned down. Cider had held up his hands like a newly-scrubbed surgeon and said, 'These fingers are going to work magic, see? But you break the spell if you watch.'

Sleep didn't really come, but he slid into a kind of timeless drowsiness for more than an hour. There was twilight in the van, with the shutter pulled down to leave a gap of a couple of feet, and he could hear the distant and muted shuffle of people passing. Even the occasional putter of a paddock bike or the strident roar of the opening event were insufficient to break through the soporific haze. The third race, twenty laps of 125cc machines, was well under way when he had the strange sensation, without any forcing or effort of will, that his senses and his powers were returning to him one by one, heightened and sharpened to a degree that he'd never felt before.

When he sat up he felt a surge of adrenalin, not the sick apprehension that he'd felt several times over the past few weeks, but a dose of pure warm energy that began deep inside and pulsed inexorably to all parts of his body. He swept back a tangle of curls from his forehead and moved to the back of the van, lifting the shutter and looking out. Julie was there, a slight anxiety clearing from her eyes as she realized she wouldn't have to pick the best time to climb in and rouse him.

'Listen,' he said. 'If you'll bring me a glass of that disgusting juice you can help me get into my leathers.'

Before the leathers came the padding. He took a couple

of sips of grapefruit juice and then put the cup aside and stripped down to his underwear. There were thick pads for shins, knees and elbows, the most vulnerable and bony points of abrasion which would suffer if he found himself in a slide. Then he wriggled into the bottom half of the brand new leathers, dark and supple with an edge stripe and a simple *Freeman* lettered down the thigh. Before he got into the upper half, Julie handed him a stiffened back support to give him some protection from spinal injury, and he fitted its shape into the small of his back before putting his arms into the sleeves and shrugging into the rest of the suit. She helped him to get the sewn-in shoulder padding seated squarely, before he drew the zip across from waist to shoulder and reached for his boots.

A couple of minutes later they were walking towards the Silver Dream bay, Nick with his bright new helmet under his arm. It was custom-fitted, like the leathers, and it had been expensive; but this time, he'd told himself, there would be no skimping, no cutting corners. This time we'll do it right.

Cider was waiting, his kit spread out and a range of spares laid ready to grab at a moment's notice. They were sharing the bay with another one-machine outfit, but there was enough room for each of them. Both end-doors of the workshop were open, making it more like a concrete tunnel; one end gave onto the pit apron, the other gave access from the paddock behind.

'Welcome to the dirty fingernail club,' Cider said proudly. 'Excuse me if I don't shake hands, but I've been giving the last couple of tweaks to Little Miss Perfection here.'

Nick nodded and smiled. 'Let's take her out,' he said calmly.

Even here, alongside bikes whose collective values would run into millions, the Silver Dream still looked special.

Other fairings were in sponsors' colours, the advertising large and easy to read over a distance; next to the cool sheen of the Silver Dream with the plain number thirty-seven they looked brash and vulgar, gaudy and tasteless.

By now the fourth race was over, the 250cc event, and out on the grid a marshal was putting down numbered cards for the guidance of the riders lining up for the 500cc race. He was getting visibly annoyed as pressmen and photographers managed to get in his way or tread on the cards or inadvertently kick them aside. Nick swung into the saddle of the Silver Dream and gave a couple of light bounces as Cider checked the catches on the fairing. It felt like home.

Mendoza's Suzuki had been acting up unexpectedly in the Trans-World bay. There was no consternation, no fuss; it was simply wheeled away by two mechanics, whilst another two brought the backup machine from the bike transporter. McBride was standing a little way apart, not his usual high-decibel self. Al Peterson pushed through to him.

'Something wrong, Bruce?' he said.

'Nothing. Just taking a look at the creeping asshole with the new machine.'

Peterson looked around, following McBride's eyes to where Nick was astride the Silver Dream and talking to Cider, who was crouched beside him looking up. Julie Prince was the other side of them.

'Oh, come on!' Peterson said impatiently. 'Forget it, Bruce! Who the hell is he?'

'He put in a good time, didn't he?' McBride said stubbornly. A couple of St John's Ambulance Brigade men walked past on their way to the Copse Corner first aid post.

'Listen,' Peterson said, 'Perry's practice time was phe-nomenal. That's what you should be worrying about – with that fluted fairing he's the fastest thing around Becketts corner I've ever seen.'

'Yeah,' said McBride, sounding less than convinced, and he reluctantly dragged his attention away from Freeman. Nichols and Mendoza were over by their machines, and when Clarke Nichols looked his way, McBride signalled and moved towards them.

'Excuse me, Al,' he said. 'Tactics.'

Peterson frowned at the exclusion as the three of them went into a private huddle a few yards away.

Cider slapped Nick on the shoulder, feeling the stiff shape of the padding under the hide. 'You listening to me, man?' he said.

Nick blinked and returned his attention from the distant conspiracy. 'I'm listening,' he said. Across the pits Mendoza turned around and looked briefly at him, trying to disguise the movement as a broad survey of the area, and then he turned back to McBride, nodding.

'I'm serious, man,' Cider was saying. 'Don't let that needle go over the line! And I mean *ever*!'

'Sure,' Nick said. 'Jets?'

'I put 320s in there to last the race. But your plugs can oil up and then you'll have to burn them clean, okay?'

'Got it.'

The Trans-World riders broke up and went back to their machines, as other bikes were being bump-started and rolled out onto the grid. 'You still listening?' Cider said.

'Yep.'

'Oiled plugs or not, never open her up all the way. She'll burn you up in sixty seconds and I'm not fooling. There's more power there than anybody ever handled before.'

Julie couldn't resist coming in. She had to raise her voice to be heard over the roar of the bikes out on the track. 'Watch it on those sharp curves,' she shouted. 'Don't get boxed in. And, Nick? I—'

Nick silenced her with his hand. 'You'll be telling me to remember not to fall off, next. Don't say another word. It's bad luck.'

He kissed her and then took his helmet. It slid on with difficulty, but once settled the moulded cheek-pieces held it firm and comfortable. A slap on the back from Cider and he was away.

McBride cruised past, all stars and stripes and Suzuki, and his visor flashed a hard look at Julie.

'Kind of like old times, isn't it?' Cider said, and Julie was able to smile.

Nick found his position on the grid, number six, and as he got into place a marshal promptly took the card away. Nick looked around, fixing the place in his mind. McBride cruised in to the number two position just ahead, and he didn't look back.

The flag went down for the warm-up lap, and the field moved forward. Nobody tried too hard because there was nothing to gain at this stage, just an easy motor round to get both engines and riders ready and pepped-up for the real competition. Riding the Silver Dream in the middle of a pack was a new experience for Nick, and he was grateful for the opportunity to get over the novelty of it; there was quite a difference from steering the Yamaha through similar situations and from speeding the Silver Dream alone around the airfield.

Nobody hit much more than seventy on the warmup, and although the group strung out for safety they kept pretty much in grid order. There were fifty bikes entered, but at least a couple had pulled out at the last minute with insuperable mechanical difficulties and one had stayed behind on the grid with a stalled engine.

McBride was not far in front, hunched down and tense, ready to give everything whether it counted yet or not. As they came out of the Abbey Curve dog-leg Nick glanced back and saw Ben Mendoza creeping along on the inside, not more than a bike's length behind. Oh no you don't, he thought, not so early, and he gave a little more throttle. The tachometer needle barely moved as he got the extra power that he needed, pulling him forward smoothly and seemingly without effort. Then it was Woodcote and the stands, and they were braking and sorting themselves out into their original grid positions again.

There was a moment's delay as a couple of argumentative photographers were hustled back from the edge-line of the track. Several of the riders looked around in annoyance, their concentration easily broken by any distraction. Nick was calm, unruffled. A few yards in front McBride didn't even seem to be aware of the disturbance.

Then the order came to dismount and stop engines. Those riders who were still in the saddle gave a last anxious twist to the throttle and then climbed off to stand by their machines. Suddenly it was silent – a heavy expectant silence which was broken by the gantry lights changing from red to green. Then the fifty were running, lumbering along with their reluctant bikes as the motors turned over and tried to catch.

The Silver Dream fired almost immediately. Perry was already away up front but McBride was still running, his Suzuki coughed sluggishly. A couple of bikes passed on either side and as Nick prepared to mount up he saw Dick Greenfield of New Zealand wobbling unsteadily across his course. Greenfield's Yamaha hadn't caught yet and Nick had to pull back; now McBride was away and a handful of other bikes were overtaking, but Nick pulled out around Greenfield and was accelerating and leaning over to the right as he moved into Copse Corner.

Cider and Julie watched him go. There were tears in Julie's eyes as he disappeared from view. Cider seemed to be rapt and apprehensive at the same time.

'There you go, baby,' he said quietly to himself. 'Long, long way . . .'

Nick guessed that he was lying about halfway down the field, but it was too early yet to worry. This was the first of twenty-eight laps, and placings and positions were likely to change radically over the next half-hour. Steve Perry was leading already and it was at this end of the field that the really hard competition could be found. None of the leaders was liable to fall back as a result of mishandling, and putting aside the possibility of engine failure any switch-around would be as the result of a finely-judged gamble on a dangerous opportunity.

He glanced down at the tachometer. The dense banks of the South Grandstands were ahead, and even on the straight at a hundred and ninety the needle was well down in the safety zone. He held his place through the short stretch between Stowe and Club corners and then, as they moved again into the long dog-leg towards Woodcote, he gave the Silver Dream a little more leash.

Sounds were deceptive as the roar from the bikes around and ahead battered at the padding of his helmet, but he could feel through his seat that the Silver Dream was absorbing the extra load without strain or effort. He passed four bikes in as many seconds and dropped into line in front of them so as not to lose his advantage on the corner.

The pits and the crowds passed as a series of flickering images, and then he was leaning hard and to the right into the second lap. He thought that he had Cider and Julie's position fixed in his mind – hell, how could you miss Cider at *any* distance in that great sea of pasty sun-starved faces? – and he filed the reference away for later use. When things began to get tight he didn't want to spend valuable time hunting for the information board, maybe even falling back as a result of wavering concentration.

Three laps, and another six bikes behind him. He could

almost hear Cider's voice in his head, 'Man, I thought I told you not to redline that needle,' and Nick told him, 'Sure, Cider, it's okay, just see for yourself.' The power kept on coming, smooth and slick and easy, and the Silver Dream was cruising at what seemed to be a mere fraction of its potential.

But speed wasn't everything. Regardless of the capabilities of the bikes the laws of physics constantly bore down on them, threatening spin-offs or slides when corners were taken too fast or too late, or even threatening to prise bike and track apart if a straight run was attacked with inadequate judgement and excessive enthusiasm. Another four fast laps saw Nick placed at the centre of a group some way behind the leaders. From now on, it wasn't going to be so easy.

'Easy,' Cider whispered as Nick went out of sight. 'Easy, now . . .'

'Talk to him, Cider,' Julie urged, her eyes trying to retain the last brief image of his disappearing figure.

'He hears me,' Cider said confidently. 'He hears me fine.'

Julie grabbed the signal board and a piece of chalk, and hastily scraped out 'LOVE' in large white letters. Cider glanced down and frowned; perhaps the situation was rather too serious for kids' games, but then he thought what the hell? Maybe it'll keep him happy. He readied his stopwatch as the pack came around again, and Julie hoisted the board to where Nick would be able to see it.

'Julie,' Cider said as soon as he could be heard over the diminishing roar of the motorcycles. 'He saw the movie too.' She blushed, amused and embarrassed all at once as she put the board down. Cider took a look at the big display scoreboard. Nick was now running seventh.

Jack Freeman hitched himself forward in his grandstand seat, as if the extra inch or so of proximity to the track would show him more of the action, would ease the flow of silent and desperate encouragement that he wanted to pour down towards his son. His glossy programme was rolled into a tight tube, and he was twisting it back and forth without even noticing. 'Come on, Nick. Come on, Nicky my boy.'

'Seventh,' Benson observed to the two Japanese businessmen by his side. He thought he was doing pretty well in keeping cool despite the little boy inside him that wanted to jump up and down, and yell and whistle, every time the Silver Dream flashed past. 'Moved up a place.'

The two Japanese looked back at him blankly. It would take more to impress them. God only knew what it would take to make them show it.

McBride took the lead from Perry. It happened coming out of Becketts Corner, Perry leaving a little too much of a gap on the inside as he righted after the curve and McBride judging the width and slipping through it in less than a second. The manoeuvre was seen from the South Stands and from the high banks along the Hangar Straight, and moments later the rest of the track heard about it through the course commentary. The scoreboard display changed accordingly.

'Say what you like,' Cider muttered under his breath, 'the guy can ride.' Then he took a quick sideways look at Julie, but she hadn't heard. He raised the watch again and waited for Nick to pass.

Still no danger from the rev-counter as Nick hunted for his opportunities to move up the pack. Nichols and Mendoza were trailing him, no longer a worry, and he could see Bruce McBride's gaudy red-white-and-blue leathers up front. He was pleased. He didn't want to see his enemy beaten down to the last in the field; second place would be the more appalling frustration, a win of exquisite finesse. Stay where you are, McBride. Stay where you are while I come and get you.

Greenfield lost his Yamaha on Stowe Corner. He thought he saw a chance that wasn't there and he blew it. He hit the bales and the chickenwire at about ninety, and the bike carried on for nearly a hundred yards before it got snagged in a growing tangle of wire and promptly up-ended itself and smashed down onto its side, breaking up as it fell. A marshal came running with an extinguisher to douse down any running fuel and prevent an explosion. The St John's men were on their way to Greenfield, and the call was already going out for the course doctor.

Parts and pieces were still spilling and rolling onto the outside of the curve as the second bunch of riders came in. Nick had only one more man to beat and then he would be able to cover the gap and get right up front with the leaders – start making his play against McBride.

The Kawasaki in front seemed to falter, decelerate slightly as the rider gave a quick sideways glance to make sure that he wasn't going to be endangered by rolling debris. Nick quickly had to abandon his bid to cut through as he was forced to fall back a little; he couldn't do a hard and fast swing out because he knew he'd collide with one of the bikes just behind his shoulder. But the Kawasaki had lost its speed advantage and was forcing him back behind it; for the moment there was nothing he could do, and he could sense the other competitors moving in around and getting ready to overhaul him in the same way that he'd passed them.

On Abbey Curve he knew that somebody had drawn level on the outside. He took a quick look. Ben Mendoza in Trans-World livery. The Silver Dream was offering him power; come on, it said, take it, there's enough to walk all over them and Bruce McBride as well, all you have to do is tell me you want it and I'll give it to you. Look at the needle, I'm not even sweating.

But the Kwacker blocked his way, and seemed unable to regain its former pace and speed. Mendoza's Suzuki pulled forward, the rear wheel drawing level with the front of the Dream and then clearing it. Nick glanced over his left shoulder as Woodcote approached; would there be enough of a gap for him to pull out and use the power that he knew was under him?

Clarke Nichols was riding on the outside line, pacing him, blocking him. And as the lap numbers changed on the display board Mendoza eased in to replace the Kawasaki.

Cider saw the lap numbers change a couple more times, and checked his stopwatch with a frown. 'What's wrong, man?' he muttered. 'Any slower, and we'll be seeing the smoke.'

Nichols and Mendoza had it well worked out – but then, they'd had plenty of practice. Few spectators could keep their eyes on any one bike for more than a couple of seconds as it whipped past, and they were sufficiently spaced for the strategy not to be obvious. Maybe the TV cameras could pick it up, but they would be concentrating solely on the leaders. The leaders were becoming more and more distant as the caged Silver Dream fell back.

Nick glanced at the needle angrily. It was way down. The two Trans-World backup riders were deliberately forcing him back, and other competitors were now overtaking easily on the outside. There seemed to be no way out; they gave him no gap, and if he tried to fall back and chance getting around on the outside they simply slowed with him and then held him there. Along with the torrent of abuse that was pouring through his mind was a question; what kind of rider was it who let himself be bought in this way? Who traded off his own competitive urges, the energy that made his heart beat and his blood flow, so that *somebody else* might be first across the line?

Bastards, that's who, came the answer. Men who would cause death because of promises dangled before them. And still they blocked him in, still they slowed him down.

Way up ahead, McBride glanced back over his shoulder. The field was way back in the distance, nobody even pushing him. Not much more than half a dozen laps to go – he reckoned he could hold on until the champagne was flowing on the big winner's truck before the grandstand.

Stay cool, Nick told himself. They want you to get angry, to get so steamed up you'll make a mistake.

One rider to win, and two to back him up. They single out the hottest contender and box him in, one in front and one on the outside, get him really mad.

Bastards.

Maybe you get him so mad that he kills himself. It's called legitimate tactics.

'Oh, God,' Julie said as the tight bunch of bikes passed the pits. 'Cider, they're doing it! They're blocking him!'

'Sure looks that way,' Cider said in a voice of tight fury.

Julie grabbed his arm. 'Stop him, Cider, please! They'll kill him!'

'*Stop* him? Baby, are you out of your mind? Nothing I could do short of throwing myself out on the track is going to do that.'

She pulled away, and for an awful moment Cider thought she was going to try running out onto the track as a serious course of action. But she grabbed the board and turned it over onto its blank side and began to chalk, in big letters, *STOP*.

'Hey,' Cider said. 'Leave that.'

'Let me go,' she said, and shook his hand off her shoulder.

'What are you playing at?'

'They're doing it again.'

'Doing what?'

'They'll kill him. I mean it, Cider.'

'They've got him blocked in, that's all. It's a lousy trick but it's just about legal.'

'They do it deliberately!' she yelled over the sound of a couple of passing stragglers. 'That's how they killed Jimmy! Cider, we've got to stop him!'

Cider looked at her hard, and he saw the truth in her eyes. Without further argument he grabbed the signal board from her and started to go over her lettering, pressing so hard with the chalk that it broke up and splintered. The average lapping time for the course was a little over a minute and a half; even with Nick being forcibly slowed it wouldn't be much more than a few seconds before he came around again.

McBride came past, out in front and alone. He was gone before the next group appeared, jockeying for second place. A long string of solo riders passed as Cider scrambled onto the low concrete pits wall and leaned against the safety rail, the signal board held high above his head where Nick couldn't fail to miss it. Nick was still caged when he appeared, dodging and manoeuvring as much as he was able in an attempt to use the bend to escape. It wasn't working.

'Come on, baby,' Cider muttered desperately. 'You hearing me now?'

He thought he saw a brief flash of Nick's visor as he streaked by. Surely he must have got the message – even without it, surely it was obvious what was being tried. He lowered the board and climbed down from the wall.

'Cider, no!' Julie said, horrified.

'I think he saw it. Don't see how he could have missed it.'

'But Cider, look!'

He looked down, and it was as if a large mass of ice had suddenly begun to descend within his chest. The board was reversed, on the back, the heavily chalked *STOP*, and on the front the message that Nick had seen.

LOVE

Nick was lying around twentieth in the field, worse than when he'd started, and with each lap the chances of recovery grew less. Nichols and Mendoza were holding him now, not forcing him right out of the back of the field – that would be too obvious – but content to keep him where he could no longer be any kind of a threat.

Bastards.

They had him tightly sewn up. He couldn't squeeze between them, and there was no way he could drop back and then pull around them.

Why not, the Silver Dream wanted to know.

Because every time we slow down they just slow down with us and keep us hemmed in. Okay, so I could brake really hard and fall back before they realized what was going on, but then we might as well say goodbye to the race altogether. If we haven't already. We'd never have the speed to get back into the running.

Try it, the Silver Dream urged him. That might be true of any ordinary bike, but I'm special. You haven't even asked me to do a fraction of what I'm capable of yet. It isn't too late – let's show them.

Okay, Nick thought, and he braked. A brief touch and the tyres bit and scrubbed on the tarmac. Nichols and Mendoza seemed to leap ahead suddenly, but by then Nick was gunning the throttle and swinging out to pass them, and the Silver Dream served up the speed without effort, and they were left standing.

Nick glanced over his shoulder as the two Trans-World riders receded into the distance, and then he checked the tachometer needle. The revs were building, not into the danger area yet but approaching it fast.

Forget the dial, the bike roared, this is what I'm *for*!

Two laps to go and the bike was diving forward, seemingly unstoppable, power building with no obvious limit. He came right along on the outside of the field and started passing one after another; no scheming, no dodging, no cutting-in, he simply put one behind him and reached for the next. The bends came and went and he barely had to slow to negotiate them. Stowe Corner, Club Corner, Abbey Curve and with Woodcote and the final lap ahead he passed the last of the bikes and there, some way ahead and closing, was the lone figure of Bruce McBride and his Suzuki.

The needle was over the line. Nick began to feel a twinge of doubt but the bike said no, there's more to spare, my heart isn't going to burst, not for a long time yet. Okay, thought Nick. Let's take him. Let's take him so everyone can see.

So they took him where everyone could see, right between the main grandstand and the pits, just as the marker was going up to indicate the start of the final lap. McBride was head-down and grinning, seeing all the people standing and screaming and thinking it was for him – and then suddenly he was just another runner feeling the buffet of the Silver Dream's slipstream. The grin disappeared and he tried to lay on the throttle, but the Suzuki was giving him everything that it had.

'He's done it!' Julie squealed with her arms around Cider. He felt her soaring joy, but he was looking at his stopwatch.

'Oh, shit, man,' he breathed, not wanting to believe what it was telling him. 'Easy, Nicky . . .'

There was the wide open track and there was Nick and there was the Silver Dream, the three interlocked to become something far removed from mundane reality. Back at the grid the chequered flag was being shaken out for their return, and then everything would begin to unwind and the grim world would start to filter in. McBride was way behind without a hope of catching them but still they ate the track faster. The annoying caution of the tachometer needle was ignored and forgotten as Nick and the Silver Dream tried to squeeze the brief moment as hard as they could to raise it to the level of an eternity and there ahead, at a steeply canted angle as they came through Woodcote at an impossible velocity, was the grid. Every detail was sharp and clear, as if Nick had broken through some barrier of conscious detachment to step back and analyse the moment at leisure; each face in the crowd was an individual to him, every shout and gesture a distinct and telling expression. The chequered flag was falling, flapping easily in the breeze. Al Peterson, his jaw hanging open in stupefied disbelief. Julie, her face streaked with tears, and Cider just behind her; but what was it that Nick read in his eyes?

The flag completed its drop, and the entire stand began to rise. We did it, Nick told the Silver Dream, and he raised both his hands in a fierce wave of victory, knowing that in their perfect partnership the Silver Dream would keep contol.

I know, said the Dream. I'm sorry, but I can't . . .

And its heart burst.

Nick felt himself going, saw the crash barrier coming for him. The Silver Dream was a slowly unfolding ball of flame moving on down the track. Maybe they'd bounced a couple of times before they parted, he couldn't tell. He almost had time to say goodbye and then the barrier hit.

EIGHTEEN

Simon Addison wound another sheet of paper into the old Olivetti portable and tried again. It was late and he wanted to go home, but he couldn't leave until he had what he wanted. Trouble was, he didn't really *know* what he wanted, and so he pecked and fretted and screwed up pieces of paper like a dog snarling and worrying at an old shoe.

He tried a sip of coffee, but it was cold. He wrinkled his nose in disgust and stuffed one of his old reject sheets into the plastic cup to soak up the dregs before he dropped it in the wastebin. Then he cracked all his knuckles and tried again.

Nick Freeman is a Grand Prix Champion who lives forever in the moment of his victory, he typed, but the paper was out of the machine and a crumpled ball even before he'd finished the sentence. Mawkish.

He sighed, and looked around the darkened office for inspiration. The pool of light that spilled over his own desk was the only bright oasis in a desert of dark shapes and paper mess. Somebody was shuffling about in the twilight on the other side of the frosted glass at the far end of the newsroom; probably Plowright, the night editor, on one of his incessant searches for fresh biros and unused paper clips to pocket and take home. In with the paper and one more time.

Today, the racing world is trying to reconcile itself to the fact that its newest and brightest star was tragically killed in the very act of his ascendance . . . Rip. Crumple. Rambling.

Addison stared out of the window at the moonless sky. The window needed cleaning, and the dirt on the glass

173

marred the clear tranquillity of the night. Wearily, he reached for another sheet of A4.

Nick Freeman cheated death and lived higher. For an instant.

He left the paper in the machine and snapped off the light. Then he took his jacket from where he had thrown it on a nearby desk and went home.

All Futura Books are available at your bookshop or newsagent, or can be ordered from the following address:
Futura Books, Cash Sales Department,
P.O. Box 11, Falmouth, Cornwall.

Please send cheque or postal order (no currency), and allow 25p for postage and packing for the first book plus 10p per copy for each additional book ordered up to a maximum charge of £1.05 in U.K.

Customers in Eire and B.F.P.O. please allow 25p for postage and packing for the first book plus 10p per copy for the next eight books, thereafter 5p per book.

Overseas customers please allow 40p for postage and packing for the first book and 12p per copy for each additional book.